Griffin Parks unknowingly crushes the hopes of more than one Hanford woman. . . .

"I intend to take up permanent residence on a cattle ranch after Christmas," Griffin said.

"You do." It was a statement, not a question, and Mama looked stricken.

Poor Mama, was all Sebbie could think as she remained seated, willing herself not to shed the tears that threatened to surface.

And poor me.

She stared at the knothole in the floorboards.

She rubbed the toe of her shoe in circles.

She stopped rubbing her toe, sat still, deathly still.

She looked over at Mr. Parks.

He was a cowhand.

Like Papa.

She remembered how her mother had draped over her father's coffin, tears running in a torrent down her face as she placed a handful of wildflowers in his stiff, gray fingers.

"Dashed dreams," Mama had wailed, "that's what killed you, Jed Hanford."

Sebbie chewed on her bottom lip to keep herself from crying. If indeed there had been a love match in the making between her and Mr. Parks, she knew with a certainty that Mama would not allow it now.

KRISTY DYKES lives in sunny Florida with her husband, Milton, a minister. An award-winning author and former newspaper columnist, she's had hundreds of articles published in many publications including two *New York Times* subsidiaries, *Guideposts's Angels*, etc. She's written novellas in three Barbour anthologies, *American Dream*, *Sweet Liberty*, and *Church in the Wildwood*. This is her first Heartsong Presents novel. Kristy is also a public speaker. Fun fact: Kristy is a native Floridian, as are generations of her forebears (blow on fingertips, rub on shoulder). She enjoys setting many of her stories in early Florida, "the last frontier" according to historians. Write her at kristydykes@aol.com or at Barbour Publishing.

The Tender Heart

Kristy Dykes

Heartsong Presents

To my hero husband, Milton, who is my collaborator in the deepest sense of the word—he's believed in me, supported me, and cheered me on in my calling to inspirational writing.

A note from the Author:
I love to hear from my readers! You may correspond with me by writing:

> **Kristy Dykes**
> **Author Relations**
> **PO Box 719**
> **Uhrichsville, OH 44683**

ISBN 1-58660-808-8

THE TENDER HEART

Our mission is to publish and distribute inspirational products offering exceptional value and biblical encouragement to the masses.

All Scripture quotations are taken from the King James Version of the Bible.

All of the characters and events in this book are fictitious. Any resemblance to actual persons, living or dead, or to actual events is purely coincidental.

PRINTED IN THE U.S.A.

one

Central Florida, 1888

For the first time, Sebbie Hanford left herself out of the count as she prepared breakfast for her mother and four sisters. The level of oatmeal in the tin canister was simply too low.

"One for Mama," she said, carefully measuring the scoop and dropping the oatmeal into the pot on the range. "One for Kit. One for Bertie. And one and a half for Ophelia and Cecilia between them."

Stirring the watery porridge, she stared out the window at the vast stretch of Florida pastureland with its understory of wire grass and palmettos, dawn's pink-and-coral aura holding her spellbound.

She looked down at the pot, fretting about their hard times. "Thank the Lord all six of us are females," she whispered, remembering her father's voracious appetite, then feeling a lump form in her throat even though it had been five years since his passing.

As she calculated how thin she would have to cut the small loaf of bread to get six slices, her glance flitted to the shelves on the wall; and she knew without checking that the canisters were empty of flour and sugar and coffee.

She dumped the last of the tea leaves into the boiling water on the back of the range and stirred the oatmeal again. Last year, they had sold the final portion of their ranch, Happy Acres, except for the parcel the house sat on. But the money from the land sale was long gone. If her sister Kit could get them a turkey or a deer every now and then and they could keep raising a few vegetables, maybe, just maybe, they could make it a few more months. Then what?

"I can get all the squirrels you could want," Kit had told them over and over. "They make a good stew. Calvin Williams says so. Or you can fry them. His family eats squirrels all the time—when they're not eating frog legs."

"No–o–o," her other sister Bertie had wailed. "You can't shoot a squirrel." Once, Bertie had caught and tamed a squirrel and carried it in her skirt pocket until it got loose and the black-and-white barn cat devoured it.

"We are not eating squirrels," Mama said every time Kit offered. "Just because we live in the wilds of Florida doesn't mean we're going to act wild. There are some things I simply won't allow."

Standing by the stove, Sebbie smiled at her five-year-old sister Cecilia as she skipped into the kitchen. She was thankful for the thought-brightening sight of the precocious little tyke.

"'We wish you a merry Cwis-mas,'" Cecilia sang, her words a lisp through her snaggletoothed grin.

"'We wish you a merry Christmas,'" Sebbie sang along.

Sebbie's mother rushed into the room, fastening the top button at her collar as she sang too. "'We wish you a merry Christmas—and a happy new year.'" She looked into the pot on the range. "Is it almost done, Sebbie? I need to leave before long. Mrs. Adams said I could display our quilts in her boardinghouse only if I arrive before the space fills up."

"I'm hoping you do a brisk business with the Northerners today, Mama."

"I'm hoping so too, Dear. I'm praying I'll sell so many quilts, I'll be able to replenish our staples and buy feed for Princess and Brownie, enough to last us at least a month."

"'We wish you a merry Cwis-mas,'" Cecilia sang again.

Her mother bent over and stroked Cecilia's cheek. "Why are

we singing about Christmas, Girlie? It's three months away."

"If I start early enough," Cecilia said, "maybe my Cwis-mas wish will come true. What's your Cwis-mas wish, Sebbie?" she lisped.

Sebbie looked down into Cecilia's cornflower blue eyes. *If only my eyes harbored the same hope that I see in yours, Cecilia.* "What's my Christmas wish?" she repeated. "Plenty of food and clothes for you, and Ophelia, and Kit, and Bertie." She ran her finger into one of Cecilia's flax-colored curls, which bobbed with every turn of her head. "And a sense of well-being and security." What they sorely lacked.

"I want a doll for Cwis-mas," Cecilia said.

A shadow crossed Mama's face. Then she seemed to rally, her fingers zigzagging across Cecilia's back. "Go wash up, Girlie. Breakfast is almost ready. And be sure to awaken Ophelia. I'm surprised she's not in here too. You twins always do everything in pairs."

"I woked up first this time." Cecilia dawdled through the door, her blanket trailing behind her.

"You woke, not woked," Mama called after her. "And tell Bertie breakfast is ready." The steady clink of spoons and knives filled the quiet kitchen as she joined Sebbie in setting the table. "My Christmas wish puts legs and feet on your Christmas wish, Sebbie, and walks it right into fruition."

"What's your Christmas wish, Mama?"

Her mother didn't answer, just kept on with her work at the table.

"Mama, I asked you. What's your Christmas wish?"

"I wish you would marry a well-to-do man and take us out of our penury," she blurted out, as if it were hard for her to say and she wanted to be done with it.

"My, what a preposterous thing to wish."

"It's. . .it's just as easy to fall in love with a rich man as it is a poor one," Mama said hurriedly.

"Even if I agreed, where would I meet such a man?" Sebbie asked.

" 'But my God shall supply all your need according to his riches in glory by Christ Jesus,' " Mrs. Hanford quoted from the Bible, her hand raised in the air like a parson, her finger pointed heavenward. "We have a need, and the Holy Book promised that God would provide." She wiggled her eyebrows up and down, like Papa had always done.

Sebbie was certain her mother was funning with her. Well, she would give her the satisfaction of joshing a little longer. Sebbie continued pouring milk into the glasses, not saying a word; but she thought about what her mother had said. It didn't matter to Sebbie if the man she married had wealth or not. To her way of thinking, there were only three things that counted. One, he must love God. Two, he must love her. Three, he must love her family as his own.

"With the winter visitors streaming in from the North," Mama said, leaning over the table to place a spoon beside the bowl, "there are many ways you can meet a rich man, Sebbie."

"You aren't funning, are you?"

"If you married a well-to-doer, think what you could give the girlies. A proper raising like I had, with social invitations . . .and an excellent education. Maybe you could provide them with travels abroad if you married well enough."

Sebbie was aghast, could feel her eyes widening. Her mother was indeed serious.

"Your papa and I had such high hopes and dreams. He and I came to Florida to prosper, and we decided that our children, when God sent them, were going to have all the advantages. But it didn't work out that way. . . ."

"No."

Mama gripped the back of a chair and looked across the table, her gaze fixed on the far wall. "My father must've known how difficult it would be to start up a ranch in Florida. I'll never forget the day your papa announced he was bringing me here. My father called Jed 'Wanderlust Jedediah.' He pleaded with us not to come. But Jed had it in his heart."

Mama was gripping the chair so hard, her knuckles were white. "We didn't listen to my father about coming here. I don't mean to put pressure on you, Sebbie, but I implore you to heed what I'm saying. I have the advantage of looking back after years and years of adversities—one after another. Years of hard living. . .and. . .hard dying. You don't have that. . .you're young. And. . .and I want the best for you. Do as I say, not as I do, as the old saying goes. My life. . .*transeat in exemplum.*"

"Let it become an example." Sebbie whispered the translation soberly, the milk pitcher tilted in midair, her thoughts far away from her task.

"Yes. An example." In two strides, Mama was beside Sebbie, holding her by the shoulders, looking intently into her eyes, slowly shaking her head back and forth. "You are our only hope. Kit's too rough and wild, and Bertie's not much better." She paused and drew in a breath. "They remind me so of your papa. The twins are going to be as beautiful as you when they grow up, and I hope as genteel. But by then, it'll be too late. They need their chance now."

Tears misted her eyes, and her bottom lip trembled as she looked pleadingly at Sebbie. "Please, Dear, heed what I'm saying," she choked out. "Marry well, so you can help us."

"Isn't there anybody in your family who could come to our aid, Mama?"

She shook her head, slow-like. "I received the same amount of inheritance as my six sisters. You know that. That's all I was due, and that's all there was—"

"Yes, and Papa invested the money in the ranch. . . ." Sebbie's words trailed off as the familiar ache grew inside her.

"On a whole herd of cattle—"

"That was killed by the cattle blight," Sebbie finished.

Mama nodded gravely. "I'm sure you'll make a wise decision, Sebbie, when the time comes." She turned and dashed across the room, mumbling over her shoulder something about making sure Kit and Bertie were loading the wagon, that it was nearly time to go.

"Oh, Mama, what are you asking of me?" Sebbie's words seemed to echo in the empty kitchen as she walked back to the stove, her footsteps leaden. She stood there, leaning against the wall to steady herself, trying to take in the magnitude of her mother's words.

"Transeat in exemplum," her mother had said. Latin for "Let my life be an example."

Sebbie felt a knot in the pit of her stomach.

"Marry well," her mother had said.

Like the waters bursting from a dam, a verse of Scripture flooded Sebbie's mind. "Honour thy father and thy mother." The words struck her with such force, her hands shook as she dished up the hot oatmeal.

Could she honor her mother in this situation? She had always been an obedient daughter, one who didn't hesitate to do her mother's bidding. But could she do what her mother was asking now? Marry a well-to-do man in order to help her family?

Sebbie smiled and playfully whopped the wooden spoon on the wall in a *rat-a-tat-tat* rhythm. "Only if God sends a man. . .riding up out of the blue."

☙

Late in the afternoon, Griffin Parks followed along behind the wagon of a certain widow lady, Mrs. Hanford. He was looking forward to a hot meal and a restful night's sleep, what she had promised him when the proprietor of the boardinghouse told him her rooms were full.

For a year he had been living on a cattle ranch, sleeping on a narrow bed in a bunkhouse—or in a bedroll under the stars. The prospect of a comfortable mattress was appealing.

In a few weeks, he would be living in these parts permanently. With the inheritance he would soon collect on his trip up north, he intended to purchase a cattle ranch a few miles due south of this part of the state.

As his horse, Marco Polo, trotted down the dusty road, Griffin's mind drifted. He wasn't sitting in the saddle, swaying with the *clip-clopping* movement of a horse, bound for a widow woman's house and a tasty dinner.

No, it was a year ago, and he was at a debutante ball in Philadelphia at the urging of his socialite mother. As he looked over a sea of satin, his heart almost stopped when he saw a particular young lady with captivating gold-brown eyes.

Miss Drucinda Hearst, *belle tournure* from New York City, stood out from the crowd with her *plaisanterie* and *esprit*. On previous occasions when he had chatted with her, she had been snide to him, rude even, displaying behavior far beneath her apparent polished cultivation.

At those earlier social events, he had felt like retorting, "My parents are thoroughbreds like yours, Miss Hearst. Haven't you heard what the stage humorists say? 'In Boston they ask, How much does he know? In New York, How much is he worth? In Philadelphia, Who are his parents?' "

Instead of making the retort, however, Griffin had summoned his inner reserves, made his perfunctory bow, and backed away from her.

So as he looked over the young beauties at the debutante ball, he decided he would make no more overtures to Miss Drucinda Hearst. He wasn't a lunkhead. He knew when a lady had drawn the curtain between them.

When he felt a tugging on his elbow, he looked down and was surprised to see a familiar captivating gold-brown pair of eyes coquettishly staring up at him.

"What a delight," she purred, "to see you here, Mr. Parks."

"A pleasure to see you, Miss Hearst." Acting like the gentleman that he was, he put aside his qualms and decided to converse with her. For close to an hour, the beautiful Miss Hearst clung to him, promenading around the ballroom on his arm, apparently proud to be with him.

"I'm going to the ladies' refreshment chamber, Mr. Parks," she cooed after a long while, her dark lashes fluttering. "You'll await me, won't you?"

"Your wish is my command." He said the gentlemanly words with a slight bow. After she flounced away, her skirts swishing, he found a seat on a silk sofa in the conversation area.

Three fresh-faced young ladies approached him and curtsied, chatted for long moments with him, then swept away. Two more did the same. Each time he stood out of courtesy, then sat back down.

Fiddling with his sapphire cuff jewelry, he hummed the song the orchestra was playing.

"That's Mr. Parks," an elderly woman's voice said from behind him, where chairs were plenteous. "Next year, when he reaches his twenty-fifth birthday, he'll inherit his grandfather's vast holdings—"

"I already know about it, Gladene. And so does everybody else who's here tonight. The word's leaked out. When his ship comes in, he'll be as rich as Croesus. He'll make some young debutante a mighty fine catch."

Griffin jumped to his feet and made long strides across the ballroom. *So that's why you're pursuing me like a hound after a fox, Miss Hearst. And that's why the other hounds came sniffing.*

He collected his overcoat and gloves and dashed down the steps of the massive mansion. *You want me for what I can give you, Miss Hearst, not for who I am.*

At the street corner, he hailed a chaise, sickened by the conniving, by her, by them all.

He would get away from this den of deceivers.

He would follow his dream and go to Florida.

He would learn the cattle business just as he had been contemplating, and then he would purchase a ranch. . . .

Now, as he followed behind Mrs. Hanford's wagon in sunny central Florida, he carefully guided Marco Polo around a cavernous rut, confident that he would soon be an independently wealthy rancher. He would have the wherewithal to survive droughts and disease, and he would restock his cattle over and over if necessary. One day, in the not too distant future, he would be shipping boatloads of longhorns out of Punta Gorda and down to the lucrative markets in Cuba.

"Easy, Boy," he whispered, leaning down and patting Marco Polo on the neck. He remembered the other momentous decision he had made the night of the debutante ball. *I will tell no one about my station in life.* So for a whole year, not one of the cowhands he had bunked with or ridden beside had found out about his prestigious family background or his forthcoming wealth.

And he intended to keep it that way.

Last week, his twenty-fifth birthday had come and gone unnoticed. Soon, he would be moving permanently to the land of sunshine, ah, sweet sunshine. . . .

two

Finished with her canning, Sebbie put the last jar of green beans on the kitchen shelf, the long row representing many months of toil in the puny garden out back.

She wiped her forehead with the corner of her apron, then looked heavenward. "Please let these beans last all winter, Lord. Multiply them, like You did the widow of Zarephath's cruse of oil and barrel of meal."

"For Cwis-mas, I want the big doll in the store window," Cecilia told Ophelia, both of them playing jacks near Sebbie's feet.

Ophelia elbowed Cecilia. "That's not fair. That doll is my Christmas wish."

"But I saw her first," Cecilia said, a tear welling in her eye, her only display of ruffled feelings. She was the mild-mannered twin.

"Did not," Ophelia spouted. "I saw her before you did."

Sebbie knelt and gathered the twins to her, one in each arm. "Ophelia, Cecilia," she said gently. "Remember what Mama said this morning? It's too early to think about Christmas. It's nearly three months away."

"We ain't never had a doll of our very, very own," Cecilia whispered.

"We haven't ever," Sebbie corrected.

Ophelia nodded in agreement, her bottom lip pushed out. "Our doll—the one you played with, Sebbie—she lost her only eye yesterday. She can't even see us no more. And she don't have no arms no more."

"Doesn't have any arms," Sebbie corrected again. She hugged

14

the girlies to her, crooning. "Shush, shush, little ones."

Cheek to sun-reddened cheek, hair to damp blond hair, she could smell the distinct scent of little girlies who had run in and out of the house all morning, never going beyond the porch, of course. They had chased the cat and finally managed to catch him, then put a baby bonnet on his head and tried to rock him in the cradle, but that only produced scratches on their arms. Then they begged for a quilt to drape over upturned chairs to make a fort, and that occupied them for awhile.

But when they had come racing into the kitchen and Ophelia had a lizard clamped onto each earlobe—dangling like ear jewelry—Sebbie had shrieked like a bantam hen and finally thought to give them six empty jars and a pan of water and the ends and strings of the beans.

"I desperately need some help with the canning," she had told them, and it kept them busy for the last hour.

Now, as she knelt beside the twins, their strong earthy odor filled her nostrils, and she drew in a deep breath, more for courage than for air.

"'Hush, little darlings, don't say a word,'" she sang, her voice a verbal caress. "'Mama's going to buy you a mocking-bird—'"

"'And if that mockingbird don't sing,'" Ophelia belted out, "'Mama's going to buy me a diamond ring.'"

Sebbie smiled, playfully pulling one of Ophelia's curls. "A diamond ring, is it?"

"No, I want a doll," Ophelia grumbled, clinching her teeth and stomping her foot at each word, five staccato taps on the wooden floorboards. "The doll in the store window."

"There, there," Sebbie soothed, at a loss for words. How did one explain disadvantaged circumstances to a child?

"I'm thirsty." Ophelia pulled away and dawdled to the kitchen table. "I'm hungry too," she whined.

Sebbie stood up and smoothed her skirts, watching Ophelia's

eyes roaming over the checkered cloth. "Supper'll be here before you know it. Can't you wait? Let's see. What'll we have this evening? Beans, bread, and fried ham. Doesn't that sound good?"

"We always eat that."

"I know." *That's what we've eaten for a week.* They wouldn't have had ham at all. They had planned to raise the sow as a brooder—had acquired it as a pink little pig when they'd traded Papa's pipes for it. The sow had just had her first heat and was ready for breeding. But then one morning a week ago, they had found her poor, mutilated carcass beside tracks that led to the nearby patch of piney woods; and they had been sickened that they had lost their fine brooder sow. There had been nothing to do but butcher her—or what was left of her. They had cooked the last shoulder ham a few days ago. Two more slices were left—tonight's supper.

As Sebbie stood rubbing her temples, she thought about her father and felt a pang in her heart. *Papa, I miss you so.* They all missed him, everybody except Ophelia and Cecilia. The twins were born a month after he was taken. When Papa was alive, there had been fried chicken fairly often and a good supply of fresh vegetables and jelly-laden biscuits. There were even occasional frosted layer cakes.

And when Sebbie was a little girl, there had been sugar cookies for Christmas, cut out in unique shapes by Mama: alligators with cinnamon-sprinkled snouts, and palm trees with clove-studded trunks, and whatever else struck her mother's fancy.

"I'm so hungry, I could eat a squirrel." Ophelia banged two spoons on the tabletop as if they were drumsticks.

Sebbie grimaced as she had seen her mother do many times. "There, there."

"And I want a new doll."

An idea struck Sebbie, one that she knew would get

Ophelia's mind off the doll she could never have. "I need to draw some water, so I'll tell you what I'll do. I'll make a little picnic, and while I'm working, you two can sit under the tree and partake."

Cecilia squealed in rapture. "You mean like dinner on the gwounds?" she lisped, clapping her pink palms together and jumping up and down. "Like we had at chu-uch?"

Sebbie nodded but didn't correct her. It wasn't a real church Cecilia was speaking of. It was a clapboard building that served as a church when a parson came through. On rare occasions, it was a social hall. The rest of the time, it served as a school—when they could keep a teacher.

"Yes, you and Ophelia may have your own dinner on the ground."

"Tra-la-la," they both cried as they spun around the room, bumping into chairs.

"Quit your horseplay if you want your treat. And go wash your hands."

Both girlies raced to the pan on the drain board and stood on tiptoes, reaching into it.

"And use soap," Sebbie said crisply. "Lots of it." She cut two thin slices of bread, slathered them with butter, and poured buttermilk into a jar. "When you're finished washing, come here and let me smell your hands."

The twins dashed to her, and she smelled their palms. Satisfied, she praised them, then wrapped the bread in a cloth napkin and picked up the buttermilk. "Come on, girlies. Let's go have dinner on the grounds." Her voice was a singsongy chirp. "Bring your cups. They're on the drain board."

With the two little girlies trailing after her, she managed to slip on her old work boots by the door. She stepped onto the warped planks of the porch and stopped abruptly, blinded by the midafternoon sun. Even though it was the first of October, it felt like a hot summer day; and she wished her hands were free so she could push her sleeves higher. She hoped it would be cool tomorrow. That's the way it was this time of year. Hot one day and cool the next.

Not anything like Massachusetts, Mama had said many times. In Massachusetts, Mama liked to say, winter is winter, and spring is spring, and summer is summer, and fall is fall, like seasons are supposed to be. But it wasn't that way in Florida land.

Sebbie made her way down the steps and across the raked yard, the girlies chattering happily behind her, and she walked on toward the laurel oak. A squirrel scampered across her path, then stopped to chomp on an acorn; and a song sparrow warbled overhead on a moss-draped limb, the wispy gray masses swaying like curtains in a breeze.

"At least we have birdsong to cheer us," Sebbie mumbled under her breath, fretting about the bare kitchen canisters once again.

After Sebbie got the girlies settled nearby with their picnic, she rolled up her sleeves, turned the crank on the well, and pulled up the bucket, being careful not to let the water slosh, like her sister Kit always did. Kit was forever in a hurry, a constant bustle of motion.

She smiled, thinking of dark-haired Kit, sixteen last month, tall and gangly, a little too loudmouthed at times, and far too active for a lady, but with a heart as big as the open range all about them.

Then she thought about redheaded, freckle-faced Bertie, fourteen on her last birthday, large-boned like Kit, but not quite as boisterous, her hands always at the ready to help, clumsy though they were.

Sebbie ached when she thought about her mother, her hair blond at one time but now streaked with gray, her eyes the same shade of blue as Sebbie's. Her mother's complexion was fair too. But there, the resemblance stopped.

She set the bucket on the ledge, leaned over it, peered in at her reflection, touched her cheek. In place of her smooth skin, her mother's was lined with worry wrinkles. Instead of her strong, straight back, Mama's was stooped and rounded from the harshness of life.

First, the ranch had failed.

Then Papa had died.

Then Mama had given birth to the twins.

Then Mrs. Boutwell, the banker's wife in town, had called Mama foolish for not giving her the babies to raise. But Mama said no, she refused to split up her family.

"Sebbie, Mama's coming," Ophelia yelled as she came running up, panting, her tiny chest heaving up and down. "I see the wagon. Way down the road."

"Maybe Mama's bwought us a pepp-a-mint." Cecilia was running too and clapping her hands. Then she stood as still as a sentinel and folded her hands in a prayer stance under her chin. "A pepp-a-mint."

"She brought you a peppermint if she sold some quilts today," Sebbie said. "Hopefully, she did a brisk business with the Northerners."

"Northerners?" Ophelia asked.

"People from up north. They come to Florida to get away from the ice and snow this time of year." Sebbie paused and whispered to herself, "I hope Mama earned enough to replenish our staples and buy some feed for Princess and Brownie, like she was hoping to do."

"A pepp-a-mint," Cecilia said, staring into the distance, hands still folded under her chin.

Sebbie stroked Cecilia's back. "And if my tatting sold well, there will be enough money to buy you girlies some shoes and maybe enough for a bolt of fabric to make you some dresses—"

"Yippee yi, yippee yay, yippee yo," Ophelia shouted,

twirling around, holding her calico skirts out sideways.

"Ophelia Hanford, you sound like a cowhand. Where did you learn that coarse language?"

Ophelia didn't answer, just kept twirling. Then she swung her arm high in the air, as if she were lassoing a calf, her little body rocking back and forth, heel to toe, toe to heel. "Come round you pardners, one by one, and grab that maverick, we'll have some fun."

"Kit taught you that," Sebbie whispered, smiling wistfully. "She would remember the old days of cattle ranching. . .and cowhands coming and going. . .and branding irons heating up. . .and cattle drives commencing. . . ."

She leaned against the well, absently toying with her chignon that was loosened from its pins, remembering when the cattle blight had come. Every last one of their herd had dropped like flies. And that's when Papa had taken sick.

"Heart ailment," the doctor had proclaimed after he examined Papa.

"Heart ailment is right," Mama said sadly, shaking her head, a knowing look in her eyes.

Sebbie would never forget what her mother had said a few months later, when she stood over Papa's coffin, tears running in a torrent as she placed a handful of wildflowers in his stiff, gray fingers.

"Dashed dreams," Mama had wailed. "That's what killed you, Jed Hanford."

"Will we weally get a new dwess, Sebbie?" Cecilia lisped.

"I want a pink one." Ophelia stopped her lassoing and walked over to the well. "With lots of ruffles and bows."

"I want lace on mine. Will you tat me some lace, Sebbie? Your lace is so pwetty."

"No, she's going to tat me some."

"But I asked first."

"Sebbie, are you listening to us?" Ophelia yanked on

Sebbie's skirts. "We want you to make us some lace."

Her mind still on her father, Sebbie felt the twins tugging on her skirts and looked down.

"Lace, Sebbie—"

"I'll make lace for both of you. Lots of lace. Yards and yards of it. It'll stretch to China."

The girlies giggled. Then Ophelia held out her skirts again. "I'm so tired of wearing brown. Brown, brown, brown."

"But it's so serviceable," Sebbie said.

"I want the prettiest pink dress in the hold white world."

"You mean the whole wide world."

"I mean I want a pink dress." Ophelia stomped her foot in the dirt.

"You want too many things, Girlie," Sebbie said softly. "Things you can't have." She looked at her own dress, an outdated blue shantung. She touched the odd assortment of buttons down the front. The bodice was wringing wet with perspiration and so thin, the outlines of her chemise would've shown through, only she had worn a blouse underneath this morning. The hemline hit her way above her ankles, and she sighed. It had been a long time since she'd had a new dress.

And her mother? For years now, her mother had reworked the dresses she brought with her from Massachusetts.

Poor Mama. What sacrifices you've made for our family.

Sebbie slowly turned the crank on the well, felt rivulets of perspiration run down her backbone. "I know one thing," she mumbled, fingering the faded fabric of her sleeve and looking down at her thin dress, "you're going into the ragbag after you've had a thorough washing."

"I have to get washed now?" Ophelia whined. "I don't want to get washed now."

"No, Ophelia, you don't have to get washed now. I wasn't talking to you."

"Mama's almost here." Cecilia was jumping, stirring up a

cloud of dust almost as big as the one on the road. Her curls jiggled and her eyes danced.

"Run to the house, Cecilia, and bring me some cups. They're going to be thirsty. And wash your hands before you handle them. With soap," she added crisply.

"Yes, Sebbie," Cecilia called as she dashed down the path.

"Somebody's with Mama and Kit and Bertie," Ophelia cried, her tiny hands cupped over her eyebrows. "I see a horse behind them, and there's a man on the horse."

"A man?" Sebbie reached for the bucket of water making its way up the well on the pulley, removed it from the hook, and put it on the stone ledge. Then she twirled around and saw a sight that jarred her soul.

A man was riding up.

Out of the blue.

three

Sebbie watched dumbfounded as her mother's wagon turned into the yard and approached the well, a tall man trotting along behind it on a huge horse.

Who was the man?

And why was he coming to their house?

She bunched, then unbunched the fabric of her skirts, deep in thought, a quiet knowing filling her heart.

Her sister Kit jumped and hit the ground running before the wagon ever came to a halt.

"Kit," Mama called, her hands on her chest, "you're putting your life in peril, as well as my heart. Haven't I told you time and again to wait until I brake the wheels?"

"Sorry, Mama." Kit never stopped, just raced across the yard.

And you're acting very unladylike, Kit. Sebbie knew that's what her mother would say if a guest had not been present.

We are ladies, and I insist on proper deportment. That's what else Mama would say, after she rolled her eyes in an attempt to hide the merriment lurking in them.

Sebbie smiled up at her mother as the wagon came to a halt. The twins were squealing like piglets and jumping up and down. From the corner of her eye, she watched in puzzlement as the man dismounted and removed his hat.

If I'd known you were bringing visitors, Mama, I would have dressed for the occasion, Sebbie thought, her heart filled with mortification. She hurriedly unrolled her sleeves and buttoned her cuffs, noticing greasy stains where little hands had grabbed her.

Clutching his hat, the man approached the buckboard and

thrust his hand upward, obviously offering his assistance. "Mrs. Hanford, may I help you down?"

"Why, thank you kindly, Sir," Mama said as she daintily alighted. The twins lunged at her; and she knelt and hugged them, burying her face in their necks, all three of them laughing and kissing as if they had been separated a month instead of a day.

"Miss Bertie?" The man extended his hand upward again.

"Thank you." Bertie picked her way down to the ground with his assistance, though Sebbie knew she usually jumped like Kit did.

"Mr. Parks, I'd like you to meet my other daughters." Mama stood and straightened the hat strings under her chin, the twins clinging to her skirts but quiet for a change, apparently in awe of the tall stranger. She smiled and gestured to one side. "This is my eldest. Sebbie."

Sebbie beamed at her mother. *Mama, you act as if you're introducing Queen Victoria to him.*

"And Sebbie, this is Mr. Parks."

Sebbie looked at the towering man. Her heart for some reason thumped hard in her chest. . .at the man who had come riding up out of the blue? She held her hand out, determined to keep her voice from shaking. "I—I'm pleased to m—meet you, Sir." She didn't succeed. Her voice was a squeaking mess.

"My pleasure, Miss Hanford." He shook her hand briefly and released it. "Griffin Parks is my name."

"Sebbie has been a great comfort to me," Mama said, "since. . .since Mr. Hanford passed on."

The man didn't say anything at first, and it struck Sebbie that it was his way of showing respect.

"What an unusual given name you have, Miss Hanford," he said. "I've never heard it before. Sebbie." He drew out the syllables, and they seemed to float from his lips. Sebbie's heart thumped harder.

"She was named after my mother," Mrs. Hanford said. "And she's very much like her, though Sebbie never had the privilege of meeting her. But Mother would've been proud of her namesake." She opened a colorful fan and waved it. "I've educated the children myself; and though I'll be the first to admit that their education doesn't equal the one I had at McGowan's School for Girls in Massachusetts, I don't mind saying that my daughters are as bright as the noonday sun. And Sebbie's talents run a wide gamut, Mr. Parks, from cooking to overseeing a household to tatting—"

"Mama, perhaps Mr. Parks would—"

"And she's gifted in the musical arts." Mama held up her hand, as if she weren't going to tolerate an interruption from Sebbie, her voice bubbling with enthusiasm. "Sebbie has far exceeded the instruction I've given her on the piano. That's the one thing I insisted on bringing when we moved here. She's mastered hymns and classics."

Sebbie held her head high, acquiescing to her mother's desires, her manners too impeccable to make a second attempt at turning the conversation. Then she glanced down at her long tapered fingers and saw her nails—jagged and work worn. She hid them in her pockets.

"Sebbie is truly a lady, like my mother was."

Mr. Parks nodded and smiled. "It's most apparent that what you're saying about your daughter is true."

"It is, Mr. Parks. It is." Mama was staring into his eyes, her tone authoritative.

"And who do we have here?" He tipped his head toward the twins.

Mama looked down at the twins on either side of her. "These little tykes," she said, touching the tops of their heads affectionately, "are our girlies. Ophelia and Cecilia."

They bobbed in curtsies. Mama smiled from ear to ear, and Sebbie knew her mother was proud of their flawless etiquette.

"My pleasure again," he said. "Only, instead of giving hand-shakes to Miss Ophelia and Miss Cecilia. . ." He stopped talking abruptly, tucked his hat under one elbow, and stooped down. With a movement so fast no one saw it coming, he reached out with both hands and tickled each of them behind their ears. "I'll give them a ticklety-ticklety-tump." They gig-gled uproariously. He touched them behind their ears again, and they giggled again. Chuckling, he tweaked them on their button noses, and even Mama began to laugh.

" 'He that is of a merry heart hath a continual feast,' " she quoted from Proverbs.

He nodded, then sobered as he stood back up.

"It appears you've been around children before, Mr. Parks."

"A long time ago," he said quietly, "I had a little sister. . .one I loved more than life itself. She saw her ninth birthday but not her tenth."

Sebbie's heart turned a somersault inside her chest. This man was not only handsome, he was gentle natured.

The man cleared his throat loudly as he looked down at Sebbie. "Miss Hanford, you're probably wondering why I'm here. The boardinghouse was filled to overflowing, and your mother offered me a room in your home."

A room, Mama? Here? Where will we put him? The bunkhouse where the cowhands used to bed down has a caved-in roof. And every bed in our house is full. Oh, Mama, what were you thinking? She squared her shoulders, swallowed deeply. No matter, they would offer him gracious hospitality as her mother had taught her all her life.

"Mr. Parks will only be here a few days," Mama said, tak-ing a step toward Sebbie, "although I assured him we would be pleasured to put him up longer."

Sebbie stared at her mother's odd gestures that she was carefully hiding from Mr. Parks—eyebrows wiggling, head tipping, eyes darting then widening. When her mother rubbed her thumb and fingers together, Sebbie was sure Mama was trying to tell her something.

I've brought you a rich man, Sebbie.

Somehow Sebbie had known that was what her mother was doing from the moment she spotted Mr. Parks sitting high atop his horse, trotting down the road behind her mother's wagon on his way to Happy Acres.

"My business will be finished within a couple of days," Mr. Parks said, "but thank you, Mrs. Hanford, for the offer of staying longer. And thank you for providing board. I'm looking forward to the tasty meals you promised."

Board too? Sebbie was aghast. She hadn't thought of food. What would they feed the big strapping man?

Little Ophelia made a clamor about candy, and Mrs. Hanford thrust a tiny, red-and-white-striped bag into Bertie's hands. "There, there, Ophelia. Settle down. You and Cecilia, go with Bertie, and she'll give you a surprise. Bertie, take the twins up to the porch and divide the treats evenly."

"A pepp-a-mint?" Cecilia cried.

"You'll find out on the porch."

Ophelia grabbed the striped bag from Bertie. "Let me carry it."

"Mind your manners, Ophelia." Mama wrested the bag from Ophelia's tight grasp and handed it to Bertie. "I'll be there shortly, Bertie."

"Yes, Mama." Bertie turned and briskly walked away, Ophelia and Cecilia bouncing on either side of her.

"May I offer you some water, Mr. Parks?" Sebbie dipped a cup into the pail where it sat on the ledge of the well. "You must be hot and thirsty."

"Water would be a most pleasant sight." He swiped his forehead with the back of his hand and reached for the cup she offered.

"And you, Mama?" She held out a second cup of water.

"Thank you, Dear." Mama took the cup and sipped. "Mr. Parks, Sebbie will take care of you for now. I must attend to supper." She walked toward the wagon.

"Most obliged, Mrs. Hanford."

At the back of the wagon, Mama stopped and picked up a large sack, squawking noises coming from it.

Chickens, Mama? For a fried-chicken dinner? What a luscious thought.

"Where is that Kit?" Mama mumbled as she set off toward the house. "Sebbie, I'll send her out directly to see to unloading the wagon."

"I'll be glad to lend a hand," Mr. Parks called. "Those boxes look heavy."

Heavy? Then the sales were good. Sebbie squelched the urge to shout, "Hallelujah" like Kit was always doing.

"I'm sure Kit will appreciate your assistance, Mr. Parks," Mama called over her shoulder. "But please, take your time with your refreshment."

"Thank you."

As the man drank like a camel at an oasis, Sebbie surveyed his appearance. He was tall and comely, and his hair was raven black. Though travel-wrinkled, his apparel had been pressed and appeared to be of good quality. She couldn't help but notice that the upper sleeves of his dark green shirt seemed to strain against his muscles, and the buttons seemed to bulge over his chest.

"Miss Hanford?" He was holding out his cup. "May I have some more?"

She looked up at him, felt her cheeks growing hot, and averted her eyes. She was certain her face was beet red, and she knew it wasn't from being in the sun without her bonnet. "Certainly." She reached for his cup with shaking hands, still not looking at him, filled it, gave it back. "Please, S—sir, drink your fill. And welcome to our humble home. Happy Acres is what Papa called it. We hope you will enjoy your stay."

"Thank you." He drank deeply and returned the cup. "I'm sure I'll meet happiness at Happy Acres."

"Your horse—" She stopped, gestured in that direction, refilled his cup once again. "He needs water too."

"Yes, Marco Polo is powerfully thirsty." He guzzled down his third cup of water. "Like I was."

"Follow me, please, and I'll show you to the house." She picked up two buckets from the ledge of the well. "And then I'll show you where to put your horse. And then I'll water him for you."

"Thank you kindly, Miss Hanford."

From the corner of her eye, she watched him put on his hat and tuck the ends of his horse's reins—Marco Polo?—into his back pocket. Then she saw him pick up the other two buckets. *How gentlemanly,* she thought.

She set out on the sandy path toward the house, being careful not to slosh. But after three steps, she tripped on a weed and walked right out of her boot—one of the worn-out work boots she had inherited from her mother, the boots she had cut the toes out of to make them fit.

She stopped dead in her tracks. *Why didn't I take the time to lace them?* Should she go on to the house, hoping he wouldn't notice that she had walked out of the boot, and come back for it later? Or should she set the buckets down and put the boot on now?

In a flash, he was in front of her with the boot in his hands, the frayed strings hanging down on either side. He knelt in the sand, almost with a flourish.

You're as gallant as Sir Galahad, Mr. Parks.

"Please," he said, "let me assist you." He pulled the tongue of the boot forward and held the sides apart.

She hesitated, hiding her bare foot behind her, more ashamed than she had ever been in her life. What must he think of her? Of them all? It was apparent he was a well-to-do man. He was well bred, his manners refined. He was a gentleman through and through, a thoroughbred. She and her mother and sisters were Florida crackers living on a defunct cattle ranch, as poor as Job's turkey.

And here she stood, subjected to the ultimate humiliation in front of this man of means, her in a threadbare dress with dirty feet and worn, holey boots.

"I used to tie my little sister's shoes." His voice was soothing as he looked up at her. "Many times."

Her face—it was heating up again.

He twisted his head away from her and looked across the vast spread of land, and she was certain he was trying to spare her further embarrassment.

Her breath—it was coming in short spasms.

"Go ahead and slip your foot in. It won't take long for me to tie it, and then we'll be on our way." He was still holding out the boot, still looking away from her. "I promise."

Her heart—it was racing wildly.

"You'll step on a sandspur if you continue without your boot." He chuckled. "I know that by experience."

"A word to the wise is sufficient," she whispered. Timidly, awkwardly, she stuck her foot into the boot. Almost without taking a breath, she watched him quickly lace only two holes, tie the strings, and then stand up. She breathed in deeply. Then she smiled.

"There," he said. "Your smile is back."

She smiled more broadly, feeling like sunshine had entered her soul. She hoped and prayed he couldn't hear the hammering of her heart as she stood there surveying the depths of his eyes, knowing he was surveying the depths of hers as well.

Finally she broke their mutual stare, her breathing still uneven, her heart continuing to pound, and turned toward the house.

"As I said, Mr. Parks, if you'll come with me, I'll show you where to take your horse. And then I'll water him for you."

four

Sitting at the supper table, Sebbie bowed her head during the blessing. Afterward, she smoothed her napkin across her lap, then held out a bowl of mashed potatoes to Mr. Parks.

He reached for it, his fingers inadvertently brushing hers as he tried to give it back. "Ladies go first."

"But you're our guest." Not only were their fingers locked, but so were their gazes. It was as if no one else were in the room, and she remembered the look they had shared that afternoon by the well. Now—as then—his look was filled with. . .

tenderness. . .

and fascination. . .

and enchantment?

Certainly it was a look that stirred her heartstrings. "Please, Mr. Parks, help yourself." She thrust the bowl toward him again. "You are our honored guest."

"If you insist." He took the mashed potatoes and spooned a steaming mound onto his plate. "I can tell someone put a lot of effort into this meal, and I intend to show my appreciation by my hearty appetite."

"I promise to have a more complete menu for tomorrow's meals," Mama said. "I'll have more time to devote to them."

"I can't think of a thing to add to this array. This looks delicious," he said, gesturing at the assortment of bowls and platters.

"This looks like Christmas supper," Ophelia piped up, her eyes darting to and fro across the bounty on the table.

Sebbie looked over the table too, and the sight pleasured her. Yes, her mother's quilt sales must have been good. There was fried chicken, the platter so full the plump pieces were

31

almost falling off the sides. A big red-and-white-striped bowl held mashed potatoes. Rich brown gravy filled a blue-flowered tureen. Peas were heaped in a yellow crockery bowl. Applesauce was mounded in a cut-glass dish. And biscuits hid in a basket under a checkered cloth. Plus, there was the grape jam Mama had bought at Hayes's General Store. They had been without sugar for so long, there was no way to make jam; and tonight seemed a festive occasion with the precious purple concoction.

"This looks like a dinner fitting for the parson." Kit was busy spreading a thick layer of jam on a biscuit.

"Looks like dinner on the gwounds to me," Cecilia said, wonderment filling her eyes.

"There, there," Mama chirped. "Bertie, please pass the fried chicken to Mr. Parks. And Kit, please pass the biscuits around. It seems they have stopped in front of your plate."

"They can stay there, if it's up to me." Kit reached for a second one, wagging her eyebrows, which made Mr. Parks smile. "Only funning," she said when Mama looked at her sharply. The girl handed Mr. Parks the bread basket.

Sebbie dipped a spoonful of applesauce onto her plate and passed the bowl, thinking about earlier when she had come into the house after watering Mr. Parks's horse. Her mother, wearing a clean bib apron and holding a stove cloth scrunched in one hand and a pot in the other, had practically shoved her toward the hallway as she delivered a passel of instructions.

"While I'm preparing supper," Mama had said, "tidy up yours and Kit and Bertie's bedroom. That's where Mr. Parks will have to stay. Move all of your necessaries into my room. You can sleep with me, and we'll make pallets for Kit and Bertie. Thankfully the twins still fit in my trundle bed. Next year, I don't know where I'm going to put them."

Mama had swiped the pot she was holding with the scrunched-up cloth. "But I don't have time to think about that now. Set out fresh towels and water for Mr. Parks, and put on clean bed linens. Then wash up the twins and see that they change their dresses. And make them put shoes on."

Her mother paused and put her hand on her hip, looking pensive. "I hope Ophelia doesn't complain about her toes hurting. Tell her I'll bring her a butter cream the next time I go to town if she won't say anything about it in front of Mr. Parks. And try your best to keep the both of them from soiling their clothes before supper. After you change, Sebbie, straighten up the parlor. And see to it that Kit and Bertie put on clean apparel too."

Then her mother had added one more instruction. "And Sebbie, Dear, please see if Mr. Parks could satisfy you. . .in a matrimonial way. Oh, I'm not asking you to agree to court him. Not by any means. It's far too premature. But what I am asking is this. While he's here, please have an open heart and please be your charming, felicitous self. After that, what will be, will be."

Now, at the supper table, Sebbie took a bite of fried chicken, feeling jittery as she glanced over at Mr. Parks. His presence seemed to fill the entire kitchen, and for some reason it unnerved her. There hadn't been a man in their house for more than a year—since they'd last served Sunday dinner to the visiting parson. She didn't remember the black-garbed minister being this. . .this big.

From the corner of her eye, she watched Mr. Parks break open his biscuit, butter one portion, and take a bite. She saw him dab at his mouth with his napkin. She watched him cut his chicken with his knife and fork. She listened to him conversing with her family, his manners impeccable. She sighed. He was. . .

polished. . .

poised. . .

and. . .perfect.

Suddenly, she realized she was giving way to thick-coming

rhapsodies of unchecked proportions. Why, she had just met Mr. Parks that afternoon. She shouldn't be thinking this way. It was unladylike and unbecoming. Inwardly, she chided herself, a line from the poet John Donne coming to mind: "*A fancy, a chimera in my brain troubles me in my prayer.*"

But then, hadn't her mother asked her to see if Mr. Parks could satisfy her in the matrimonial way? Hadn't Mama asked her to have an open heart concerning him? Oh, she was so confused.

She looked over at him, saw him pick up his glass and take a swallow, noticed how big his arms were. There was that word again. *Big*. Her glance traveled up his shirt—this time a crisply pressed indigo blue serge—to his chiseled jaw above his black string tie. Her gaze wandered to his gentle smile, which revealed even white teeth—

"Sebbie, I asked you to refill the water glasses twice now," Mama said.

Sebbie pushed her chair back so hard, the legs raked across the floorboards. "I'm sorry," she managed to say, thoroughly embarrassed as she made her way across the kitchen. What was wrong with her? Her mother had bragged about her being a lady, and here she was practically gawking at their visitor.

"When did you move to Florida, Mrs. Hanford?" Mr. Parks asked as Sebbie refilled his glass.

"Twenty-one years ago. Sebbie was born the year after we came."

"Florida-born and bred." He looked up at Sebbie as she poured water into Kit's glass.

Sebbie felt her senses tingling at his nearness. She finished pouring the water and took her seat. "My sisters and I were all born here, Mr. Parks. We are Florida-born and bred, as you call it."

"There'll come a day when that will be a rare thing."

Sebbie glanced his way, wondering what he meant.

"The state has such vast expanses—and undeveloped places, like in the southern tip—it'll never fill up. People will keep streaming into it from other states, long after we're dead and gone."

"Because of the warm winters, you think?" Mama asked, her eyebrows raised. "People fleeing the snow and ice?"

"That too. But far more important are the vast business opportunities." He stopped buttering the biscuit he held, put down his knife, and stared at the far wall. "Commercial logging, phosphate mining, the citrus industry, the—"

"Papa always said cattle ranching was the best," Kit piped up.

❧

Two hours later, dishes were done, evening chores were completed, and they were gathered in the parlor. Sebbie sat at the piano playing "Jimmy Crack Corn" at Mr. Parks's request, while he sang gustily along. As her fingers raced across the ivories, she glanced around the room, drinking in the pleasant scene, memorizing every detail.

Ophelia and Cecilia were on either side of Mr. Parks, sitting on the divan, singing along with him. Kit was in a straight chair drawn up close to him, belting out the lyrics in her off-key, tone-deaf way. Bertie was seated on a rug at his feet, humming. Mama rocked quietly nearby, her hands busy with the sewing in her lap, a contented look on her face.

Spinning yarns. Singing ditties. Popping corn. Sebbie smiled. That's what Mr. Parks had done for the last hour. And he had occasionally knelt at the fireplace, tending a pan of corn while he regaled the girls with stories and songs. Then he passed out the hot corn along with the chocolate bonbons he had produced, the rare treat eliciting a peal of glee from the girlies.

When he held the bonbons out to Sebbie and looked intently into her eyes, she had to will herself to hold her gaze steady. There was that enchantment again. *Oh, Mr. Parks. . .*

Now, sitting at the piano, she played the last bars of the lively tune and finished with a flourish of notes.

"*Bravissimo.*" He applauded vigorously, the twins giggled, and Kit and Bertie applauded too.

"Didn't I speak a truth, Mr. Parks?" Mama tipped her head in Sebbie's direction. "She's talented, wouldn't you agree?"

"Most assuredly."

Sebbie picked up the lamp on the piano, crossed the room, set the lamp on a table beside the divan, and sat down in the chair by her mother.

"You are a *virtuoso,* Miss Hanford." Mr. Parks's eyes seemed to light up. "An *artiste.*"

She felt her cheeks burning. She wasn't used to compliments. Especially from men. Especially from Mr. Parks. "Thank you," she said softly. "I enjoy my music."

"That is evident."

Silence reigned.

She smoothed the folds of her dark blue dress. She picked at the lace on her collar. She fiddled with her chignon. She wished the twins would make some noise, but they didn't. They just sat beside Mr. Parks like little statues, looking up at him adoringly. It was clear he had won their hearts. And hers? She tugged at her collar again.

"Tell us another story," Ophelia cried, pulling on Mr. Parks's elbow. "Please?"

He tweaked her on the nose, then looked at Mama. "Is there time for one more story before bedtime, Mrs. Hanford? Or is it growing too late?"

"I don't want to go to bed now," Ophelia grumbled, stomping her foot on the floor. She tugged on his elbow again.

"We've all the time in the world, Mr. Parks," Mama said. "Please tell us another story. This is a special night. *Vogue la galère!*"

"Latin, Latin, Latin," Kit piped up. "Mama's always speaking Latin."

"I like Latin too," Mr. Parks said. "But that phrase isn't Latin. It's French."

"Yes," Mama said. "It means 'row the galley.'"

"Galley?" Kit asked, a blank look on her face.

"A galley is an old type of ship, low to the water, that was primarily driven by oars," Mama explained. "Galleys were used for war and trading. You can picture a sea battle during which the order would be given, *'Vogue la galère.'* No matter what happened, the rowers were to keep the ship going. So over time, the sentence came to mean 'keep on, whatever may happen' or 'keep on, come what may.'"

"Come what may, Mama?" Bertie piped up, her brows knit together.

Mama gazed intently at Mr. Parks, then at Sebbie, then back at Mr. Parks. "Yes, let come what may." She drew out the words, placing equal emphasis on each one.

"Ouch." Kit swatted at her neck. "That mosquito bite'll leave a rising on me for sure."

"Tomorrow morning, Kit, you and I must repair the window screens," Mama said.

"I'll be happy to lend a hand." Mr. Parks inched forward on the divan, looking distracted as he stared at the torn screen across the room, lightly thumping his bottom lip with his index finger.

"That would be most kind of you," Mama replied. "Now tell us your tale, Mr. Parks."

"It happened several months ago," he began. "I was in a town in South Florida known for its outlaws. I checked in at a lodge and walked up a long, dark stairwell to my room."

A slight breeze blew through the window, and the lamp on the table sputtered and cast eerie shadows on the wall.

"Soon," he continued, "it was bedtime, and I went to bed

fully dressed so I would be prepared for anything." The resonance in his voice rose and fell at just the right intervals for effectiveness, Sebbie decided.

"The last thing I remember before I fell asleep was seeing the moon shining through the window and hearing a dog bay in the distance." He barked like a coyote. "Then I was in dreamland." He shut his eyes and made snoring sounds, and the twins laughed.

Sebbie smiled at him, couldn't keep from smiling at him.

"All of a sudden. . ." Excitement gushed from his voice. "I heard someone pounding on my door." He rapped on the low table in front of him.

Ophelia and Cecilia snuggled closer to him, and Kit leaned forward in her chair.

" 'I'm hungry,' voices at the door shouted. 'Let me in.' But I said, 'I'm too tired to get up; and besides, the innkeeper would be the one to get you something to eat. Go ask him.' But they kept yelling that they were hungry and wanted in. 'We'll find a way,' they said, and their voices sounded sinister."

"Were you afwaid?" Ophelia asked.

"Grown men don't get scared," Kit reprimanded.

"Yes they do," Mama whispered, a faraway look in her eyes. "Yes, they most certainly do."

Sebbie stared at the floorboards at her feet. Was Mama thinking of Papa, when the cattle blight came and he was so worried?

"And grown women get scared too," Mama added gravely.

Sebbie chewed on her lip. Yes, Mama had been thinking of Papa. But now she was thinking of herself, Sebbie was sure. Mama was afraid for their future. She was probably thinking about the kitchen canisters that were full right now but would eventually be empty, and she was probably pondering on the pitiful garden out back. . . .

"Kit, wouldn't you be frightened if you heard banging on

your door in the middle of the night?" Once again, Mr. Parks rapped loudly on the table in front of him.

Kit nodded and swallowed hard.

"I'll have to admit that I was apprehensive," he said. "And then I heard scratching." He shuffled his feet on the floor. "And the door handle started jiggling. . . ." He rattled a drawer pull on the table.

Wide-eyed, Ophelia covered her mouth with her hands.

"Finally, they burst through the door."

Ophelia and Cecilia let out little gasps. Kit swallowed hard. Bertie started biting her fingernails.

"Standing there, right in front of my eyes, were two of the biggest mosquitoes I ever saw."

Ophelia and Cecilia giggled uproariously, and Kit and Bertie had you're-trying-to-fool-us-but-you're-not-succeeding looks on their faces. Sebbie could feel herself glowing.

"Those mosquitoes dragged me out of bed and pounced on top of me. One mosquito said, 'Yum, yum, he looks mighty good.' But I shouted, 'You can't eat me. I'm covered with clothes, and besides that, I've got my boots on,' and he said, 'That doesn't matter a lick to us,' and the other mosquito said, 'Yes, we sting cattle right through their hooves, and we torture alligators right through their hides.'

"Then those two mosquitoes picked me up and flew down the stairs with me between them. I said, 'Where are you taking me?' and they said, 'To the swamp.' Then the first mosquito said to the second mosquito, 'You know, Jack, if we take him to the swamp, some of those big mosquitoes are liable to take him away from us. We better eat him right here.'"

Ophelia and Cecilia jumped up and down in front of him, their eyes dancing.

"And those two mosquitoes did just what they said. They ate me alive." He grabbed the twins, one in each arm, stood up, and swung them through the air. "How about that, Girlies?"

They shrieked in delight, the three of them locked in a tickle-tussle. Kit and Bertie dashed to his side, pulling on his arms, and more laughter followed.

Mama smiled, looking as pleased as the peacocks that used to roam the yard.

Sebbie's heart beat hard in her chest, and she sat clasping and unclasping her hands, watching Mr. Parks romping with her sisters. "Girlies," he had called them, using their affectionate family nickname; and she took note of it, and it touched her deeply.

The galley of my heart is not only loosed from the shore, Mr. Parks. It's in the wide-open seas. Yes, it's ready, come what may.

❧

After Bertie left the room to put the twins to bed, Sebbie settled back in her chair in the quiet stillness across from Mr. Parks, basking in her secret musings, reveling in their implications, knowing how much they would please her mother.

Could Mr. Parks be the man to fulfill Mama's wish? The thought pleased her—no, thrilled her. Absently, she picked at the lace on her collar, then fiddled with her chignon. This morning, her mother had quoted, "But my God shall supply all your need."

Sebbie kept fiddling with her chignon. God certainly knew the Hanford family had dire needs. Was God supplying them in this unusual method? Through the means of a rich man, namely Mr. Parks? Her mind flitted to the months ahead, when the canisters in the kitchen would be bare again. Was God's provision going to be manifested in this way, through Mr. Parks entering their lives?

Was she willing to do her part, if this was God's plan? Was she willing to marry him?

That's not a bad thought. In fact, it is most pleasant.

A Scripture verse loomed up in her mind, as bright as the

flame in the lamp; and she said it inside her heart. *"Not my will, but Thine, be done."*

She folded her hands, their busyness at rest, her heart at peace. Silently she prayed, *However Thou choosest to meet our needs, Lord, I am willing.*

She looked over at the tall, handsome, perfect man and for the second time that day resisted the urge to shout, "Hallelujah." God had not only supplied their needs, He had given her the desires of her heart; and she was glowing—again.

Mama closed her sewing box and rose to her feet. "Come, Kit, it's time for us to retire. Sebbie will follow in a little while. Sebbie, you'll come in a few minutes?"

"Yes, Mama."

As Kit got up from her chair, Mama strode toward the door. With her hand on the knob, Mama pirouetted, as if a thought had just struck her. "Mr. Parks, earlier you asked us how long we've lived in Florida. You've already told me this evening that you were born and bred in Philadelphia and that you haven't been in Florida very long. May I ask you a question?"

"Certainly, Mrs. Hanford."

"What brought you to this neck of the woods, as the locals say?"

"Well, for the past year, I've been living here."

"Here?" Kit asked, shoving a handful of popped corn in her mouth as her big strides made clacking noises across the floorboards. "Where's here?" she said, only it came out, "Whus huh?"

Mr. Parks smiled. "Florida. I've been living on a cattle ranch. The Double C."

"You are a cowhand?" Mama gripped the doorknob tightly, her knuckles white, her face ashen.

He nodded. "Have been for a year."

"But your apparel—"

"For months, this cowhand's been saving up the money he

earned, especially since the nearest town was too far away to spend it." He touched his sleeve. "I purchased this shirt at the general store this very morning."

"You did?"

He nodded.

"But your knowledge of Latin, French. . .your deportment. . ."

He looked pensive. "When I was growing up, my mother insisted that I learn the social graces, much as you've done with your daughters."

Mama remained silent, morosely silent.

"I intend to take up permanent residence on a cattle ranch after Christmas."

"You do." It was a statement, not a question; Mama looked stricken.

Poor Mama, was all Sebbie could think as she remained seated, willing herself not to shed the tears that threatened to surface.

And poor me.

She stared at the knothole in the floorboards.

She rubbed the toe of her shoe in circles.

She stopped rubbing her toe, sat still, deathly still.

She looked over at Mr. Parks.

He was a cowhand.

Like Papa.

She remembered how her mother had draped over her father's coffin, tears running in a torrent down her face as she placed a handful of wildflowers in his stiff, gray fingers.

"Dashed dreams," Mama had wailed, "that's what killed you, Jed Hanford."

Sebbie chewed on her bottom lip to keep herself from crying. If indeed there had been a love match in the making between her and Mr. Parks, she knew with a certainty that Mama would not allow it now.

And neither will I. I will honor my mother, as the Good Book says.

five

Griffin stood in front of the washstand and plunged his hands into the bowl, then slathered his face with water and soaped it, readying himself for breakfast with the Hanfords. He had spent three days with this frolicsome family of ladies, delighting in their warmth and affection and cordiality, and he was loathe to leave them. But it was time to go, and he hurried with his ablutions.

Peering into the mirror, he ran the straight edge of the razor along his jaw. He was impressed with the Hanfords' gentility. Even after they found out he was a ranch hand, they had treated him graciously, like an honored guest; and he couldn't help admiring every last one of them, down to the twins.

He finished shaving and washed the remnants of lather from his face and dried it, unable to get his mind off the Hanford women.

Mrs. Hanford. A more charming hostess couldn't be found anywhere, with her flawless manners and her wit as sparkling as a Florida spring.

Miss Kit and Miss Bertie. Striplings with spirit. Bonny girls, is what his Scottish valet would call them.

Miss Ophelia and Miss Cecilia. Dainty little damsels with sunshiny dispositions—well, Cecilia anyway. He smiled at that last thought.

He pulled on his shirt, buttoned it, and tucked it in.

Miss Hanford. He had reserved her until last to ponder over. . .and savor. Miss Sebbie Hanford was lovely, with her crown of pale hair and blue eyes and feminine shape. But she was more, much more. . . .

As he sat on the bed, leaned over, and put on his socks and shoes, he felt himself smiling. Miss Hanford had grit and determination, pluck and courage. She had her mother's sense of humor. And Kit and Bertie's spirit. And Ophelia and Cecilia's daintiness. And she had her own unique character trait, a compliant attitude.

"Yes, Mama, I'll do it," she had said every time her mother gave her a directive.

"I'll do it right now," she always added, her hands of helpfulness at the ready, quick to please with her tender heart.

He felt a shiver of nervousness go up his spine, stood up quickly, and placed his belongings in his carpetbag. He remembered something else that had happened last year, shortly after the incident with Miss Hearst.

"Lord, help me to find a wife," he had prayed.

He fastened the leather straps on his carpetbag, recalling a verse in Proverbs. " 'Whoso findeth a wife findeth a good thing,' " he quoted aloud. "Lord, I don't want just any wife, but the wife Thou hast prepared for me."

He stood up, set his carpetbag on the floor, and stared out the window a moment, stroking his chin. When he first arrived at the Hanfords' home and Miss Hanford had given him water from the well, then offered to water his horse, he'd had to take a deep breath to steady himself. Her actions were right out of the book of Genesis when Rebekah had offered water to a stranger, then satisfied his thirsty animals.

Griffin's glance flitted to the disarray on the washstand that needed tidying. "Hurry up, Pardner," he said aloud as he strode across the room to finish his tasks.

Wring out the cloth. Miss Hanford. There she was again, and he smiled at the ethereal vision.

Hang up the towel. Miss Hanford. " 'Many daughters have done virtuously,' " he quoted, " 'but thou excellest them all.' "

"Mr. Parks?" a small voice said through the door.

"Yes?" In a flash, he was in front of the door and swung it open. There stood little Miss Ophelia Hanford in her brown dress, two meticulously sewn patches dotting her full skirts. He tweaked her on the nose, and she giggled.

"How are you this fine morning, Miss Ophelia?" he asked as she stepped into the room.

She frowned, then brightened. "I'll be doing real good after I eat."

"Why is that?"

"Mama said Sebbie's fixing a breakfast that would outfit a king."

He threw his head back, chuckling heartily. "You mean fit for a king. Where's your mother, by the way? I need to speak with her." He needed to pay her for room and board.

"She's getting ready to go to town." Ophelia's brow furrowed and her bottom lip pushed out. "And she's not taking me this time either."

"She's going back to town? This soon?"

"I heard her tell Sebbie she didn't get her buying done the last time she was there."

He nodded, remembering. "She was wanting to hurry home and prepare supper." *For me.* "That was the day I came here."

"Mama said she's going to town today to buy material to make me and Cecilia some dresses. I want the prettiest pink dress in the hold white world. With lots of ruffles and bows. And Sebbie's going to tat me some lace to go on it." She touched her sleeve. "I ain't never had a pink dress before. All I ever get to wear is brown, brown, brown."

He smiled. "Brown is very becoming to you, Miss Ophelia—"

"And I heard Mama tell Sebbie that she's going to buy me and Cecilia some shoes." She stuck out her bare foot and wiggled her toes, and he laughed again. "My shoes pinch something awful, but Mama told me she'd give me a butter cream if I promised not to tell you." She clamped her hand over her mouth, looking guilty. "Oops."

"I promise not to reveal what you told me. After all, it was an accident. Now, what are we having for breakfast? You said it's fit for a king?"

Her pale blue eyes lit up like the aquamarines his mother always wore, reminding him of Miss Hanford's eyes. "We're having eggs and grits and biscuits. Plus hotcakes with syrup. And Sebbie's making you some cinnamon rolls to take with you."

"My, my."

"We haven't had cinnamon rolls or hotcakes in a long time." She looked down at the floor. "I forgot what they taste like. . . ."

A pang hit him in the heart.

"I heard Sebbie say she's fixing preacher comforts this morning."

He laughed again, couldn't help it. "You mean, creature comforts, Miss Ophelia." He stroked his chin, remembering all the creature comforts he had been privileged to have throughout his entire life. A fine home on a prestigious avenue. Exclusive schools. High-society hobnobbing. Trips to Paris every few years.

He rubbed the back of his neck, envisioning the Eiffel Tower, the *Champ de Mars*, the *Tuileries* Gardens. He stared down at a little girl in a tattered brown dress, and another pang hit him in the heart.

"I'm sure your sister's cooking will be better than the fare in a French café," he said softly.

Ophelia skipped across the room and pointed to a small cedar chest near the foot of the bed. "Do you know what this is?" She touched the lid caressingly, then glanced up at him, looking guilty again. "I'm not allowed to look in this box unless a grown-up is in the room with me." She smiled. "You're a grown-up, Mr. Parks, so that means I can open it."

She opened the chest and peered down inside.

He looked in too and saw shimmery folds of white. Fabric?

"This is Sebbie's silk. I heard Mama say it costed a lot of money. Mama's mama ordered it from England on the day Sebbie was born."

"Because your sister is her namesake?"

"That's what Mama said."

"You overhear a lot of things, don't you?"

Her aquamarines were full of mischief, and she nodded vigorously. "Mama says I have big ears, but I don't think so." Tugging on one tiny pink ear, she reached down and closed the lid of the cedar chest. "Do you think I have big ears, Mr. Parks?" She didn't wait for an answer. "This silk is for Sebbie's wedding gown."

"Wedding gown?"

She jumped up and spun like a top, holding out her brown skirts. "I heard Mama say as soon as she can find a rich man, we're going to have a wedding around here."

The blow hit him hard.

In the heart.

six

After breakfast, Griffin returned to his room, gathered his bags, and headed outside. He intended to saddle Marco Polo and then tell the family good-bye. He had already paid Mrs. Hanford for his room and board.

He reached the barn and stepped inside. He stood for a moment in the barn's dim light, his eyes focusing on Sebbie where she sat on a low stool, milking the cow, the tinny sounds of milk hitting the bucket and *rat-a-tat-tatting* in the quiet stall.

The vaporous vision of Miss Hanford that had enraptured him earlier appeared before him now, only it rankled him this time.

Ophelia had told him, "I heard Mama say as soon as she can find a rich man, we're going to have a wedding around here."

He kept standing there, watching Miss Hanford lean into Brownie's side, working the teats at the precise angle to get a steady stream of milk, a practiced art, he knew. Brought up in the city, he'd never milked a cow until a year ago. He saw Sebbie lean closer to the cow, and suddenly, the tinny sound stopped, and he wondered.

He craned his neck to watch her. She aimed the milk at her mouth, and a stream of the foamy liquid shot toward her, and she swallowed it. Then she resumed the milking, the tinny sounds filling the barn once again.

With the tail of her apron, she dabbed the foam off her lips. Then she laughed, the vibrant musical sounds filling the barn.

He felt like hugging her to him. But what about Ophelia's ominous words? Should he be wary? He remembered a certain young beauty at the debutante ball, the one with the captivating gold-brown eyes, the devious Miss Hearst.

He hesitated.

Forewarned, forearmed?

Was Miss Hanford like Miss Hearst?

A woman looking for a man only for what he could give her?

No, surely not. Miss Hanford had no way of knowing his background. But he was a strong, robust man, he had to admit, capable of making a good living. Perhaps that's why they were so kind to him. Were they trying to snare him?

He rubbed his jaw, deep in contemplation. He thought of Miss Hanford again with her crown of pale hair and blue eyes and feminine shape, her grit and determination, her pluck and courage, her sense of humor, her vibrant spirit, her daintiness, her helpful hands, her compliant attitude, her tender heart.

Fortune knocks once at every man's door. But before he could take another step toward her, one more niggling doubt assailed him. *Is there a way to be absolutely sure of her intentions? To prove if they are untainted?*

He heard Marco Polo whinny, and he looked in his direction. Perhaps there was. He ran his hand over the smooth leather of the saddle that hung on the wall beside him. Yes, perhaps there was.

He took a step toward Miss Hanford, his gait sure. He would do what her mother had said in French.

What was that phrase? His mind raced through a litany of terms, discarding familiar French sayings, moving on to the expression Mrs. Hanford had used the night he arrived at Happy Acres. *Vogue la galère?* Yes, that was it.

Row the galley. That's what he would do concerning Miss Sebbie Hanford. Let come what may.

With a little planning of his own involved.

❧

"Miss Hanford?"

Sebbie heard Mr. Parks's low lilting voice in the barn, and she accidentally kicked the milk pail, almost knocking it over. She looked up and saw him standing near his saddle across the barn. She had been so engrossed in her chores, she hadn't noticed him coming in. "Y—yes, Mr. Parks?"

"May I have a word with you before I leave?"

"Certainly." She stood up, wiped her hands on the towel that hung from her waist, and walked toward him in the dim light of the barn. What did Mr. Parks want with her, specifically? She knew he was leaving this morning. She was expecting to say a hospitable good-bye with the rest of the family, but she certainly didn't expect him to look her up privately.

As her footsteps fell across the soft, straw-filled dirt floor of the barn, her heart beat hard within her chest, and she silently reprimanded herself.

Hadn't she made a firm resolve the first night of Mr. Parks's stay? When he had revealed that he was only a cowhand? She would never forget her mother's reaction to that information as long as she lived.

Now, in the barn, she covered the last few steps between her and Mr. Parks, to where he stood by his saddle on the wall.

He's only a cowhand, Sebbie reminded herself. *Just like Papa. And being a cowhand had killed Papa.*

She felt her eyes misting over as she remembered the decision she had made the first night Mr. Parks was at Happy Acres. She would honor her mother and her wishes. She would not encourage Mr. Parks in any way, shape, or form. In fact, she had determined that night that she would have no further communication with him. She wouldn't even converse lightly with him. And she had kept her resolve, except for polite comments at mealtimes. She had steered clear of him for the three days he had boarded here.

As she covered the distance between them, then stopped

in front of him, a sadness overcame her. *I must force myself to forget you, Mr. Parks. As soon as you take your leave.*

Mr. Parks lifted his saddle from the wall. "So, Miss Hanford, you like fresh milk?"

She could feel her face flushing. Had he seen her sneak a sip of that wonderful warm froth? Had he seen her abandon her ladylike ways and become a. . .a hoyden for a moment? She bristled. It had been done in secrecy. He had no right to invade her privacy.

"At breakfast this morning, I noticed you drank a second glassful of milk."

She breathed easier. "Oh, yes." She swallowed hard. "We. . . we hope you enjoyed your stay at Happy Acres, Mr. Parks," she said for lack of anything better.

He nodded. "I've decided I'm a prophet."

"A prophet?"

"Someone who foretells the future."

"I–I don't follow you."

"Remember? The first day I arrived, when you welcomed me, I said I was sure I would meet happiness at Happy Acres."

She felt her face growing warm again, and it flustered her that it kept doing so.

"I did," he said.

"You did what, Mr. Parks? I–I'm not following you at all this morning." She fiddled with her chignon.

"I found happiness at Happy Acres."

"Oh." She too had found happiness at Happy Acres during his stay. But she'd had to dash it as quickly as it sprung up in her heart.

"Yes, I found happiness at Happy Acres, Miss Hanford."

What was his meaning? It seemed she was having a very hard time catching his meaning about a passel of things, and it flustered her even more.

He stepped into the stall beside his horse, and Marco Polo whinnied a welcome. "The girlies are like little dolls." He heaved the heavy saddle onto the half wall, then began brushing Marco Polo's coat with a firm stroke. "And Kit and Bertie are as fun-loving as they can be. Very enjoyable to be around." He continued brushing at his horse briskly. "And your mother, she's as regal a lady as ever I've seen."

Sebbie clutched at her collar.

"You should be proud of your family, Miss Hanford." He threw a blanket over Marco Polo's back.

She nodded. "Thank you for your kind words, Mr. Parks."

"You're welcome." He paused. "Miss Hanford, I've a matter to discuss with you. A business proposition, really."

"Then my mother is the one you need to see."

"You're the one I wish to speak to."

She stared at his broad shoulders as he saddled Marco Polo, heard his gentle gibbering to his horse, smelled the scent of soap on his person, her heart beating in double time all the while. Why couldn't he saddle up pell-mell and gallop away into oblivion? Every minute he stood there, so near yet so far away, was torture for her. He was unattainable. That was her irrefutable decision.

"The matter concerns my horse." He tightened the cinch on Marco Polo's wide girth, taking his time. "Will you board him for me while I travel by train up north?"

She was troubled. Board his horse, he was asking? She remembered her declaration.

I will not encourage Mr. Parks in any way. And more than that, I will have no further communication with him. And most important of all, I will force myself to forget him.

If she boarded his horse, she could keep none of those resolves.

"My business up north shouldn't take long."

No, she could not—would not—board his horse.

"I plan to return to these parts in a month's time."

Mr. Parks was coming back? Here? In a month? Her heart leaped into her throat. During his stay at Happy Acres, she had heard him say something about coming back to Florida to live. But was he coming to this area of the state? She hadn't understood that part. And he was coming back so soon? A month from now?

He talked on and on, but it was as if she didn't hear a word he said. She rubbed her temple where it throbbed. If only he would mount Marco Polo, leave, and never come back. Otherwise, how would she be able to rid her heart of these fluttery feelings?

Her mind ran away with her as she contemplated Marco Polo's needs. He was the finest piece of horseflesh she had seen in a long, long time. To keep him would be a big undertaking.

Mr. Parks continued talking, something about Marco Polo's feed and exercise and care.

She rubbed a crater in the dirt with the toe of her worn work boot.

"I'll pay you well, Miss Hanford. Very well."

She blinked hard. What did he just say?

"I said, I'll pay you well," he repeated, as if reading her thoughts.

She stared at the rough barn siding as if transfixed. He would pay her well? Visions of abundance filled her mind. Canisters overflowing with coffee, sugar, and flour. Ham hocks hanging in the smokehouse. Chickens clucking in the yard.

Her thoughts ran wild again, only not about Marco Polo. Then she corralled herself. Mr. Parks was a cowhand, not an Admiral Crichton, as she had mistakenly thought earlier. Still, a cowhand's horse was his most important commodity. Everybody knew a cowhand took good care of his horse, no matter what the expense. And even though Mr. Parks wasn't wealthy, he was an honest man. Somehow, she knew that. He would pay her and pay her well for her services, of that she was certain.

"Marco Polo needs—"

"I'll do it," she blurted out, stepping toward him and patting his horse on the flank.

"My, my. Such eagerness will endear you to this man." He tipped his head in the direction of Marco Polo, patting him in the same place she had just done, up under his mane. His eyes danced with merriment. "Marco Polo will be so loyal to you, he won't want to leave you when I return, Miss Hanford."

"I'll treat him well, that I can promise."

Soon, final arrangements were made for Marco Polo's care—Mr. Parks telling Sebbie of his horse's specific needs and Sebbie taking it all in. He gave Sebbie some money for Marco Polo's first week's feed supply, and they decided he would wire the same amount each week until he returned. They also agreed that they would correspond so he could keep tabs on Marco Polo and his care. Upon returning and retrieving his horse, he would pay Sebbie—generously he stressed again—for her work.

After consulting with the rest of the family, they arranged for Kit—who was accompanying Mama to town that morning—to ride Marco Polo back to Happy Acres after Mr. Parks boarded the train.

"I'll pay you generously for this favor, Miss Kit," he had said when she agreed to ride his horse back to the ranch. "When I wire your sister the second installment of feed money, I'll include your pay."

"Kit will be glad to help you out," Mama replied, showing her usual hospitable ways. "But there's no need for payment."

"Riding Marco Polo will be reward enough," Kit had said, her eyes glowing with excitement.

A half hour later, the family stood in the yard bidding Mr. Parks adieu. More arrangements were quickly made. He would tether his horse to the hitching post at the depot, he told them, and then he would board the train. Kit could find Marco Polo there.

As he put on his hat, the girlies begged him to swing them in the air as he had done on his first evening at Happy Acres, and he twirled them around and around. And then Kit and Bertie got in on the action, giving him hearty handshakes and calling out overzealous good-byes as they climbed in their mother's wagon.

Last, he said a fleeting good-bye to Sebbie, and she said one to him likewise. He mounted Marco Polo and tipped his hat to her. *"Veritas praevalebit,* Miss Hanford," he called, high on his steed.

Sebbie stood there watching him follow her mother's wagon down the road. "A Latin phrase, Mr. Parks?" she said quietly. "What are you trying to tell me? *Veritas praevalebit?* What does that mean?" She would look it up, for certain.

She gazed long and hard as Mr. Parks turned into a cloud of dust, heard with a sharpness of ear the beat of the horse's hooves that matched the beat of her heart, tried not to think about him and. . .

his polish. . .

his poise. . .

and his perfection.

She willed herself not to ponder his engaging personality. "But at the moment, I'm not meeting with success," she told herself sadly as she turned and dawdled toward the house. "That's all I am thinking about, Mr. Parks: how wonderful a man you are."

She called to the girlies to come up on the porch, dashed up the steps, and went inside. In the parlor, she searched through her mother's Latin dictionary. When she found the entry, she put her finger in the page to mark it, carried it to the divan, sat down, and opened the thick volume.

" 'Truth will prevail,' " she read from the entry. She turned the phrase over and over in her mind but could make no sense of it. " 'Truth will prevail'? What does Mr. Parks mean?"

She arose, put the dictionary back on the shelf, and turned toward the kitchen.

"Work awaits—as always."

❧

"You done well for yerself, Boy," Griffin mumbled cowhand-style as he trotted toward town, smiling, recalling the trail jargon he had picked up in the last year. Even though Mrs. Hanford and her two daughters Miss Kit and Miss Bertie were riding in the wagon ahead of him, he knew the thudding hooves on the dusty road and the rumble of wagon wheels would prevent them from hearing his silly ramblings.

"You're a right smart young feller. You laid yerself a fail-proof plan. *Veritas praevalebit*. Yes, truth will prevail concerning Miss Hanford."

He prided himself that he had strategized well. First, he would write her, presumably about Marco Polo. This would provide him the opportunity to keep in contact with her and thereby get to know her. As they corresponded, he was certain he would find out many aspects about her character. Second, he would return to these parts within a month, retrieve Marco Polo, and take a room at the boardinghouse for awhile, further extending his contact with her. Third, he would ask about Miss Hanford in town—discreetly of course—and find out everything he could about her, as well as the rest of the Hanford family.

Yes, he had laid his plans with precision. He would observe Miss Hanford at as many social occasions as possible, and he would watch her with shrewdness.

Then, once she had proved herself—and her intentions— he would. . . What would he do?

Well, that remained to be seen.

" 'Oh give me a home,' " he sang lustily, " 'where the buffalo roam, where the deer and the antelope play.' "

He paused, thinking of the ranch in Florida he would soon be purchasing. "Well, Lord, all I want is a home, like the song says. But I don't care about the buffalo, deer, or antelope."

He sang on. " 'Where seldom is heard a discouraging word, and the skies are not cloudy all day.' "

What words would Miss Hanford write in her letters? Surely they would be uplifting and sunny, like the song talked about, as she herself appeared to be.

But a more important question loomed in his mind, and he mumbled it as he trotted along.

"What does the future hold?" He longed for the day he would be living permanently in Florida as the proud owner of a cattle ranch. But he also longed for a wife—the woman the Lord had prepared for him. Was Miss Hanford that woman?

Well, that remained to be seen too.

seven

Over the next week, Griffin and Sebbie exchanged letters in quick succession.

Dear Miss Hanford,

Thank you for agreeing to board Marco Polo. With him in your care, he will do well, I'm certain. That is one less worry on my mind these days. Business affairs, you understand. Please remind Miss Kit and Miss Bertie that they may ride him as often as they like.

I had a most pleasant trip up north. If all goes as I'm antici-pating, I will return soon, hopefully in a month's time. I trust the sum I gave you will cover Marco Polo's feed for now. As we agreed upon, I will wire the same sum each week until I return. When I retrieve Marco Polo, I will pay you for your labors.

Yours,
Griffin Parks

❧

Dear Mr. Parks,

I am glad you had a pleasant trip. I've never ridden on a train, but it is something I would like to experience. My mother's people hail from Massachusetts, as she mentioned, I believe. I would be thrilled to visit them sometime, though my dear grandparents are long deceased. But my mother has six sisters, and I would be pleasured to meet my aunts.

Sebbie put down her writing pen. From where she sat at the table, she stared out the window at the oak tree beyond, the yeasty scent of baking bread wafting through the kitchen.

She toyed with the end of the pen. She could not, would not write that when her grandparents passed away, her mother had given her inheritance to Papa to restock the ranch. Then the cattle blight came, and all was lost.

A sad wistfulness washed over her. If only, if only, if only. . .

No, she would not allow herself to think of the past. She was writing Mr. Parks—a welcome thought—and she picked up her pen with eagerness.

Marco Polo is doing well, you will be pleased to hear. I thank you for the confidence you placed in me to watch over your prized steed. I have discovered that he likes carrots and apples.

"Though we rarely give him either one," she said aloud—mournfully—her pen in midair. "The children's needs come first, you see. . . ." Yet again she toyed with the end of her pen. "Only the Lord knows how much longer we can keep the wolf from the door."

She put pen to paper.

As I promised you, Mr. Parks, I will take excellent care of Marco Polo.

She stopped writing for a moment, thinking this through. Though she wasn't as knowledgeable about horses as some, particularly prize animals like Marco Polo, she was confident she could do a good job with Mr. Parks's horse. And Kit would help her, she knew. Kit was good with horses—as well as with all animals. And Bertie too.

You can put your trust in me, Mr. Parks, to see that Marco Polo fares well. I'm sure he will be horse-happy here at Happy Acres.

With sincerity,
Sebbie Hanford

❧

The second week, Mr. Parks wired money for feed, and Sebbie thanked the Lord when she received it. It was just in time, the level in the feed bag ever dwindling in the care of the mighty Marco Polo.

More letters passed between them.

Sebbie recounted a few tales of Kit and Bertie riding Marco Polo. She told Mr. Parks about the day they put the twins atop his broad back and rode them in circles around the yard, much to their delight. She recounted the afternoon the girls braided Marco Polo's mane into at least a dozen pigtails and tied them with colored hair ribbons, and how they plaited his forelock, and how she'd had to make them brush it all out again and not leave him in that fix.

He wrote about the choosing of Marco Polo's name, an intriguing story that made for amusing reading, one she read aloud to the entire family that evening, much to their delight, a story that they begged to be read over and over. . . .

> *Dear Miss Hanford,*
>
> *I mentioned I would tell you why I chose the name Marco Polo for my horse. You see, Kublai Khan, grandson of Genghis Khan, the Mongolian general and statesman, conquered China in the 1200s and became the first emperor of the Mongol dynasty. Few people impressed Kublai Khan until he met Marco Polo. Marco Polo was a Venetian traveler and explorer, and his account of his travels to Mongolia became the chief Renaissance source of information on the East. When I first read about Marco Polo many years ago, what impressed me the most about him wasn't his explorations or his conquests or even his writings. It was the fact that he told the great Kublai Khan about Jesus Christ. . . .*

❧

Sebbie wrote Mr. Parks about the morning Marco Polo reared,

"a sight to behold," she said, the thoroughbred stallion's fine mahogany coat glistening like flames in the sunlight as he pranced about the pasture on his hind legs.

He spoke of cowhand tales and trail rides and the hardships of ranch life.

She wrote of the contrast between Marco Polo and their horse, Princess. Princess was sweet-natured and gentle, she penned. Marco Polo was fine-spirited and noble with his beautiful form. He was strong of limb and seemed to glory in his speed.

The third week, he wired her feed money just like he said he would, and as before, she thanked the Lord. Food for her family was hard enough to come by, let alone horse feed.

She wrote of the day Kit took to jumping Marco Polo, a log first, then a large tree lying in the field that had been struck by lightning a few years ago. Each time, she wrote, her heart nearly failed her for fear. The day Kit jumped Marco Polo over the fence, she thought she would faint. But Kit and Marco Polo managed well, she told him.

Sebbie came to anticipate Mr. Parks's letters with eagerness. But she felt guilty as she read each one with relish. Was she being disloyal to her mother and her wishes? Surely not. This was a business matter. Yet each time she opened Mr. Parks's letters, her heart went all fluttery, and she couldn't seem to control it.

A month had passed, and she wondered why Mr. Parks hadn't returned as he said he would. But it wasn't her concern, she reasoned. He would be here any day, she knew.

Meanwhile, she set herself to continuing her competent care of Marco Polo.

eight

Sebbie stood at the fence and watched Kit high atop Marco Polo, galloping across the pastureland. Having this fine piece of horseflesh had provided her sisters some good times, and she was grateful. They were sorely in need of pleasantries, all of them.

Kit was growing attached to Marco Polo, with his spirit and his beauty; and Sebbie hoped her sister wouldn't pine for the thoroughbred when Mr. Parks claimed him. In fact, she worried for Bertie too. Bertie loved Marco Polo almost as much as Kit did.

As Sebbie's gaze followed Kit and Marco Polo across the vast field, she remembered with a skip of her heart what her mother said every time Kit jumped down from the wagon while it was still in motion, before her mother had a chance to brake. "You're putting your life in peril as well as my heart," her mother would say time and again.

That's how Sebbie felt now, as she watched Kit driving Marco Polo harder and harder and faster and faster across the field.

My, that horse can fly; and dear me, Kit, you don't have a fear in the world.

Fretting, she wrung her hands nervously. "Kit!" she called loudly, "slow down." But evidently Kit couldn't hear her.

She shook her head back and forth, trying to remind herself that Kit was good with animals. "But she's so young," she whispered, her eyes fastened on Kit and Marco Polo as they flew like one across the field. "She's had no experience with steeds of this stature." Pits and gullies littered the field, and a hoof in a wrong spot. . .well, she wouldn't let her mind run there.

Marco Polo was a magnificent creature, galloping with an easy gait, his mane and tail flying straight back in the wind, his lean muscled body stretched out parallel to the ground.

"Kit!" she yelled again.

Marco Polo suddenly halted in midstride, swung his fore-legs high in the air, and balanced on his back hooves. He came down kicking like a wild bronco and bucking too. In moments, he lost his balance and fell. Kit shot off him like a ball out of a cannon, flying through the air like a rag doll and landing in a heap in the grass.

Sebbie thought she yelled, but maybe she didn't. All she knew was she was flying herself—over the fence and then through the pasture, trying to get to Kit. Marco Polo was nowhere to be seen, not that she was thinking of him. Her only intent was to get to poor Kit. She just had to get to her, and she raced onward.

Kit was nearly covered in dirt when Sebbie reached her. She was struggling to get up, but Sebbie told her to be still, and she obeyed. Tears came to Sebbie's eyes when she saw Kit's face. Angry-looking scratches were everywhere, and her upper lip was swelling fast.

"Oh, Kit!" Sebbie dropped to her knees, not knowing where to touch, where to give a soothing pat. Kit looked so. . .so bad. Her arm had a long bleeding gash from where she had grazed a stick that was still protruding out of the ground, waving like a clock pendulum. Field grasses and thorns were stuck to her everywhere, from her moplike hair to her petticoat and stockings.

"Oh, Kit. . ." Sebbie felt faint with fear, but she knew she must buck up. Kit needed her. She took a deep breath; but still, she couldn't help the thoughts that played havoc in her mind. Kit with a broken leg. . .or worse, a back?

"Marco Polo. . .must've stepped. . .in a rut." Kit could barely be heard, her breath short staccato puffs. "That's what. . .made him fall."

Sebbie nodded soberly, took Kit's hand in her own, looked into her sister's eyes, and prayed as hard as she'd ever prayed in her life.

Mama seemed to appear from out of nowhere, and Bertie and the twins too, Sebbie saw, and they were all crying. Mama fell on her knees and elbowed Sebbie out of her way—from a mother's need, Sebbie knew—leaning over Kit, putting her cheek to Kit's, crooning softly to her.

"I'm. . .not dying," Kit said, her voice as weak as a kitten's as she struggled against her mother, trying to get up.

"Please don't move, Dear." Mama gently released Kit from her hard hug. "Let me check you over."

"I'm a little banged up, Mama," Kit whispered. "That's all."

Her mother didn't respond as she busily went over Kit's body with firm, loving hands, inch by inch, testing bones, asking questions, checking for more abrasions. When at last she judged Kit to have no broken bones, she gave quick orders for the girls to help her get Kit in the house.

"You'll be as sore as rising tomorrow, Kit. But you'll live. You'll be abed a few days too, I'm sure." Mama looked heavenward, her tone grave. "Thank You, heavenly Father, for Your protective care over my girl."

❧

Two hours later, Sebbie served supper to the family, Kit taking hers on a tray in bed, Bertie staying by Kit's side and refusing to eat—why, Sebbie did not know.

Bertie had seen to Marco Polo after they got Kit settled inside. Bertie had chased him down; and by then, he was calm, she told Sebbie later, and thoroughly ready for a rubdown, which she gave him, so vigorously and so long that she had to be coaxed into the house at supper time.

Later, while doing the dishes, Sebbie and her mother talked about the accident.

"Well, Kit took a hard fall," Mama said, washing the last plate and handing it to Sebbie, looking contemplative, "but I'm grateful the mishap was as mild as it was. When I think what could have happened—Kit crippled or even killed. . ." A sob escaped her lips, and Sebbie threw down her drying cloth and wrapped her arms about her mother.

"Oh, Mama, I know, I know."

They hugged for a long moment, then slowly pulled out of each other's embrace.

Mama reached into the dishwater, retrieved the dishcloth, and wrung it out. "But for the grace of God. . ."

Sebbie nodded. "Thank You, Lord," she whispered.

❧

The next afternoon, Sebbie was on the porch churning butter when she heard her mother scream out her name.

"Sebbie!"

Sebbie jumped like a jackrabbit, dropped the paddle, and dashed from the house toward the sound of her mother's voice. What was the matter? Her mother yelling—so uncharacteristic of her ladylike ways—could only mean one thing. . .

Trouble. Bad trouble. Sebbie's nerves were as tight as a clock spring after yesterday's ordeal with Kit, and she didn't think she could stand any more trouble.

What was the matter? Was something wrong with her mother? Bertie? The girlies? Dear Lord, no—

"Sebbie!"

The cry came again—from the barn, Sebbie determined—and she ran across the yard and dashed into the barn's cool dimness.

"It's Marco Polo," Mama cried, worry lines creasing her forehead.

"What do you mean?" Sebbie asked, breathing hard from her strenuous run.

"I'm sure of it."

"Sure of what, Mama?"

"Marco Polo. He's. . .he's limping."

"Limping?" Sebbie stopped short, feeling sick to her stomach.

"He's limping." There was gripping finality to Mama's tone. "I put him in his stall." She tipped her head sideways.

"Limping. . ." Sebbie's mind raced with wild thoughts. Limping meant lameness. *Kit! Oh, Kit, your foolishness caused you to have a sore body and Marco Polo a lame leg.*

"What's wrong?" Bertie came running up, her chest heaving. "I heard you scream, Mama."

"Where are the twins?"

"They're with Kit. She's reading them a book in bed. I just left them and was on my way out to the pasture to bring in Marco Polo—"

"What I told you to do earlier, young lady. What I've just done."

Bertie looked embarrassed, stared at the ground. "I–I. . ."

"I had to leave my work to do your chores, Bertie. But there's no time to address that issue now. Marco Polo is limping."

"Limping?" Bertie looked up at her mother, her face flushed. She tugged on her collar—over and over.

"I was bringing him in from the pasture when I spotted it. He's clearly lame."

Sebbie couldn't respond, couldn't even think. She wrung her hands. She bit her lip. She resisted the tears that filled the back of her eyes.

"He must've suffered an injury during the accident yesterday," Mama said. "We never thought to check him—we were so worried about Kit."

"Kit." Sebbie nearly spat out her sister's name, so consternated was her spirit, so grieved was her soul at this awful turn of events. "We told her over and over to take care with Marco Polo. We told her repeatedly not to ride him so fast. We told her again and again. But did she listen? No. If she hadn't been driving him so hard yesterday, he wouldn't have stumbled and lost his footing. Now. . .now Marco Polo's lame, and. . .and what if. . ."

Sebbie stopped short with her rumblings, couldn't say the dreaded words "put down," couldn't voice them at all. "Oh, Mama, what are we going to do?"

Bertie burst into tears.

"Bertie?" Mama was at Bertie's side in a flash. "What's this?" Tenderly, she brushed Bertie's cheek with the back of her hand.

Bertie fell to her knees on the hard-packed dirt floor, and her tears ran in a torrent down her face. She slumped down in front of the barrel at her side, leaned over it, and buried her face in her arms, wailing.

Mama crouched down by Bertie and put her arm around her. "Dear, what's the matter? You can tell Mama."

Bertie cried harder. For long moments, all that could be heard in the silent barn was Bertie's muffled sobs coupled with her mother's gentle crooning.

At last Bertie looked up through tear-stained eyes. "I'm the cause of Marco Polo's lameness, not Kit," she said with a steady voice. "I knew it yesterday, right after the accident."

"Whatever do you mean, Dear?"

"Marco Polo didn't stumble in a rut. I was there. I saw the whole thing. He shied at something in the field, something I left on the ground. He bucked and then. . .and then. . .he lost his footing. And now he's lame."

"What did you leave on the ground, Bertie?" her mother asked softly.

"A–a dishcloth—"

"A dishcloth?"

"I'll never forgive myself for being so careless—"

"Whatever are you talking about?"

"Yesterday, after noon dinner, I went out to the pasture to bring him in, like you told me, like you do every day. On my way, I scooped up a couple of pieces of apple from the table and wrapped them in a dishcloth. I figured Marco Polo deserved a treat."

Bertie's tears started up again. "After I fed him the apple slices, I guess I dropped the dishcloth in the field. Then Kit asked to ride him before I took him back in, a quick spin around the pasture she promised, and I told her she could. I was watching them flying over the field when it happened. The wind kicked up, and the dishcloth fluttered, and it must've scared Marco Polo, because that's when he bucked." She buried her head in her arms again. "I can say I'm sorry a thousand times, but it. . .it won't help Marco Polo." A great sob hit her, and her shoulders shook in spasms. "I deserve to be horsewhipped—"

"Nonsense," Mama interrupted, her voice stern. She lifted Bertie's chin and stared straight into her eyes. "Bertie, you made a mistake. That's all. I've never punished you—or any of my girls—for a mistake. Only for outright disobedience. And those times have been few and far between. For that, I praise God." She pulled Bertie to her in a tight embrace. "No, there'll be no punishment doled out here. We're setting our attention on Marco Polo. All of us. We're going to find out what's wrong with him, and then. . .and then. . .we're going to get him well."

nine

Three days later, after all their ministrations, Marco Polo was no better, and Sebbie was past the point of concern. She was downright fearful. As she washed the supper dishes that evening, she thought about all they had done to help Marco Polo since discovering his limp.

First, her mother had instructed Bertie to walk and trot Marco Polo on a loose lead rope while she watched him closely so she could determine which leg was lame. He threw his head up when he stepped on the sore leg and down when he stepped on the good leg.

"It's his right hind leg that's lame," Mama had said.

Next, Mama had examined Marco Polo's affected leg carefully, running her hands down it, feeling for heat, she said, or swelling, and looking for cuts or bumps. There was no sign of anything of that nature; and though puzzled, she was grateful.

Then, Mama and Bertie had carefully cleaned out the frog and sole of his hoof with a knife, looking for a wedged stone or a nail.

"There it is," Mama had proclaimed, relief in her voice. "A stone." She turned to Bertie while Sebbie and the twins looked on, a smile lighting her face. "Bertie, you didn't cause the accident. This," she proclaimed, holding up the irregular-shaped stone, "is the culprit. He stepped on the stone, it lodged in his hoof, and he bucked from the pain."

Bertie's eyes teared up as she hugged her mother. "Oh, Mama, I'm so sorry for poor Marco Polo, but I'm so glad to know I didn't cause him this trouble. I love him so much."

"I know you do. We all do. And he'll soon be well. He's got a small puncture, but salve should do the trick."

Now, Sebbie dried the last dish and hung the towel on a nail. "But the salve didn't help, Mama," she whispered to herself in the quiet kitchen, sorely grieved. "Marco Polo's worse."

❧

Four days later, Sebbie received a letter from Mr. Parks. In his missive, he apologized for his delay in coming. "Business affairs," he said. Could she keep Marco Polo a few more weeks, he asked? He was certain that nothing else would prevent him from returning to Florida. Would she be willing to help him out in this way?

Sebbie sat in the parlor rereading Mr. Parks's letter. She stared into the yellow flames in the hearth. Fall had finally brought a nip in the air, and this chilly November evening was made more bearable by the warm fire. She smiled. Probably tomorrow it would be warm once more.

She pulled her chair closer, knowing she should go to bed as the rest of the family had done an hour ago. But she had to answer Mr. Parks's letter. Her mother was going to town first thing tomorrow, and she would ask her to post it then.

All morning and all afternoon, Sebbie had tried to find time to write, but it had been too busy. It had rained the day long, and the girlies were forced to be inside the house, and she had to be creative to keep them occupied and out of each other's hair.

Now was the first time all day she could find a moment to write to Mr. Parks. She fretted over the wasted lamp oil, but it couldn't be helped. She would hurry.

She picked up her pen and wrote a line.

Dear Mr. Parks,
  Of course I will help you. The girls and the girlies are enjoying Marco Polo.

Her conscience assailed her, and she scratched out the line and balled up the paper, lamenting over the waste. She started again, determined to get it right this time. Then she paused. Should she, could she tell him about Marco Polo's trouble?

Her stomach churned as she agonized about the matter. If she did tell him, he would be angry—and rightly so—that she had not kept her word about taking good care of his horse. If she didn't tell him and Marco Polo got better before he returned, he would never be the wiser.

If she did tell him. . .

If she didn't tell him. . .

The words played havoc in her mind. What to do? What to say?

And even more important than the issue of telling or not telling Mr. Parks in a letter was Marco Polo's situation. She grieved for the animal, the finest piece of horseflesh in the world, to her way of thinking.

Would Marco Polo get better? It had been a week. Would his puncture wound ever heal?

Tears came to her eyes. In the barn late that afternoon, she had approached Marco Polo's stall with a carrot. His usual joyous neighing and frolicsome capers didn't greet her. Instead, he kicked violently, then threw his proud head back and gave an angry whickering, his eyes wild with pain.

If only Marco Polo had remained healthy in her care. . .

If only he hadn't gotten the puncture wound. . .

If only she could consult a farrier. . .

She drummed her fingers on the hard wooden surface of the arm of the chair.

"If only I could consult a farrier?" she said, the thought sounding as foreign as if she'd said she wanted to take tea with Queen Victoria. It was simply impossible.

"Lord," she prayed quietly, "please help me. I feel so troubled. I feel all confused inside."

She picked up the Bible on the table beside her, opened it, and flipped through the pages, then stopped at a book-marked passage.

" 'If any of you lack wisdom,' " she read from James chapter one, verse five, " 'let him ask of God, that giveth to all men liberally.' "

She looked heavenward. "Thank You, Lord," she whispered, suddenly feeling at peace. "Thank You for the comfort of Your Word. I'm asking You for wisdom, Father, and I'm believing that You will grant it."

With a sigh, she glanced at the letter she had started to Mr. Parks. She arose, picked it up, and headed for bed. She would have to finish it early in the morning.

As she crossed the wide hallway, walking softly so she wouldn't disturb her family, she pondered over her dilemma.

She didn't know what would happen to Marco Polo.

She didn't know what would transpire concerning Mr. Parks.

She didn't even know what she would do regarding all of this.

But one thing she was certain of.

God would give her wisdom. And God would intervene, somehow, some way.

ten

Griffin sat in the fine leather chair in his lawyer's ante-room in Philadelphia, awaiting his appointment. The male law clerk had told him it would be a few more minutes, and then he had bent over a pile of papers on his desk, leaving Griffin to his thoughts, or reading, or perhaps even a catnap.

Griffin preferred his thoughts. He stretched his long legs out in front of him, thinking of the delightful Miss Hanford down in Florida

Miss Hanford.

He remembered the day he'd left her at Happy Acres and how he had laid precise plans. He would write her, he told himself, presumably about Marco Polo. But his real mission would be to find out as many aspects as possible about her character and her family.

Well, he had written her all these weeks, and he had discovered a lot about her. But the next thing on the agenda was to go to Florida, live at the boardinghouse for a time, and observe her closely.

No matter that she was wonderful and charming.

No matter that he was drawn to this beautiful young woman with the tender heart.

No matter that he had amorous feelings for her—yes, amorous.

No matter that a warm glow seeped over him every time he thought about her.

He would still require that she prove herself and her intentions to him. He had to do this because of what had happened with the debutante. He desired for a woman to love him for himself, not for what he could give her.

At the jangle of the bell on the outer door, signaling a man taking his leave from the lawyer's office, a startling realization dawned on Griffin, and it deeply disturbed him.

He was replicating the disdainful actions of the debutante when they had first met.

He was the one standing in judgment.

He was looking on the outside, just as Miss Hearst had done to him.

It was only when she thought she could benefit from him that she had paid him any mind.

He remembered a verse of Scripture: " 'For man looketh on the outward appearance, but the LORD looketh on the heart.' "

He smote himself. That was exactly what he was doing with dear Sebbie.

He was looking on her from the outside.

But no more.

Lord, forgive me, he silently prayed.

He would accept her at face value, for who she was.

Into his being dropped the quiet affirmation that her intentions were indeed pure. He knew she was without guile. And he knew that he loved her, really loved her.

"Sebbie. . ." A deep peace settled over him as he whispered her name. As soon as he arrived in Florida, he would ask Mrs. Hanford for permission to court Sebbie. And everyone knew that courting was the precursor to proposing, so she would know exactly what he was asking. Sebbie would know too, once he began to woo her.

He would court her well.

He would treat her like the angel that she was.

He would lavish his affections on her, his ladylove.

He would give her the moon and the stars if that's what she wanted.

And along the way, she would come to love him as much as he loved her.

"Amor gignit amorem," he whispered. "Love begets love."

Yes, he would woo her, and he would win her.

A hundred images filled his mind.

Proposing to Sebbie. . .perhaps on Christmas day?

Wedding Sebbie. . .perhaps in front of her friends and certainly her family.

Living with Sebbie. . .in an abode of love.

"Mr. Parks," the male law clerk said from where he stood near the inner door. "Please follow me."

Today, this afternoon, he would purchase a ring for Sebbie. *"Who can find a virtuous woman? for her price is far above rubies,"* he quoted silently.

"Mr. Parks? Did you hear me? I said to follow me. Mr. Miller is waiting."

"Yes, yes, of course." He rose from his chair, gathered his hat and gloves. *I'll purchase a ruby for Sebbie, surrounded by diamonds in a setting of gold.*

eleven

Sebbie awoke refreshed, the troubles and cares of the previous night swept out of her mind as surely as a good spring-cleaning took care of cobwebby corners.

" 'Weeping may endure for a night, but joy cometh in the morning,' " she quoted from the book of Psalms.

Smiling as she lay in bed, she stretched, then stretched again, her arms high over her head, joy filling her soul.

She climbed out of bed and walked to the window, being careful not to awaken Kit and Bertie, asleep on the wide bed against the far wall. She would let them continue their slumber a few more minutes.

She lifted the curtains and peered out. Would it be warm today instead of cold and rainy like yesterday? By the feel of the air in the room, she knew the nippiness had dissipated some. She had a feeling that today would be bright and pleasant.

In her soul anyway.

As she washed and dressed, hurrying so she could fix breakfast, she contemplated the strange dream she'd had. It wasn't a clear image, just a fuzzy one, but she was definitely a bride in the dream.

A bride?

That brought a trembly feeling inside; but she thrust it away, trying to decipher her dream. She was wearing a beautiful gown fashioned from her wedding silk. There was no church, no groom, no flowers, no attendants, no minister. Only the gown created the dominant impression.

"I wonder why I dreamed about wearing a wedding gown?" she whispered as she brushed her hair, then twisted it into the high chignon she always wore. "If you have a wedding gown, you usually have all the trimmings, yet none of those were in my dream."

Shoes on and shawl donned, she made her away across the bedroom with a shrug of her shoulders. Breakfast beckoned—at least the making of it. She hadn't decided if she would eat or not. The canisters were almost bare again.

She remembered the letter she had started late last night to Mr. Parks. She'd better get it now, she decided, and finish writing it, then take it to the kitchen to give to her mother. That way, she wouldn't forget it later in the hustle and bustle of her mother's getting ready for her trip to town.

The letter in one hand, she grasped the doorknob with the other, then glanced back, ready to call Kit and Bertie from their deep slumber. The cedar chest in the corner caught her eye and seemed to beckon to her.

"My wedding silk," she said softly. She walked over to the chest and knelt in front of it, feeling compelled to open its lid, something she had not done in ages. There was simply no need to look at it over and over again. She knew what was in the chest, that it was waiting for the day she could take it out and cut dress parts from it.

As she opened the lid, she saw her beautiful wedding silk. Almost reverently, she ran her hand across its shimmery folds, back and forth, back and forth. She reveled in its satiny softness, then bent and smelled its sweet cedar scent.

She stood up and drew it out, held it to her chest, the long end of it still in the box. She dipped her chin to hold it there, caught handfuls at her waist, stepped to the right, saw herself in the mirror over the washstand.

Into her mind popped the image of Queen Victoria and her regal robes and her royal diadem and her silver scepter. Last night, as she was writing to Mr. Parks, Queen Victoria had flitted through her mind. But why? She tapped on her bottom lip, trying to recall the moment. Ah, yes. Now she remembered.

She had been worrying about poor Marco Polo, grieving over his plight, wishing with all her heart that she could consult a farrier, yet knowing that was as foreign-sounding as taking tea with Queen Victoria.

Then she had prayed and asked the Lord for wisdom, knowing with a surety that He would grant it. After that, she went to bed and dreamed a dream.

About her wedding silk.

Now, as she looked down at the luxurious lengths draped over her figure in tucks and folds, she rejoiced again that she—Sebbie Hanford on a defunct cattle ranch in central Florida—owned a piece of silk this fine and wonderful.

"This must be worth its weight in gold," she whispered. All of a sudden, she knew why her dream was about her wedding silk. It was as clear as the daylight that was fast breaking through the clouds and streaming into her bedroom.

"I'll sell my wedding silk and use the money to hire the farrier." She said it not loudly, but not softly either. Just assuredly.

"God has answered my prayer," she said, that same joy surging through her soul. "He's given me wisdom, what I sorely lacked late last night."

As she folded her wedding silk and put it back into the cedar chest with great care—this would be her last handling of her fine heirloom—she silently prayed, *Thank You, heavenly Father, for letting me know what to do in my dilemma.*

She looked out the window to the left where the barn stood, its weather-beaten boards shining silver in the morning light. "Marco Polo," she said softly, soothingly, "help is on the way."

She turned toward Kit and Bertie where they lay in bed— Kit stretched to her full height, her toes big bumps under the covers, Bertie snuggled against her like a newborn babe.

"Hallelujah!" Sebbie shouted, Kit-style, smiling from ear to ear.

Kit sat up with a start and rubbed her eyes. Bertie came flying up beside her, rubbing her eyes too.

"Hallelujah!" Sebbie shouted again, this time laughing.

"What's all the racket for?" Kit asked sleepily.

"You mean, why am I shouting 'hallelujah,' like you're always doing?" She smiled broadly. "It's an expression of thankfulness to the Lord, you know."

❧

Sebbie tapped on her mother's bedroom door. "Mama?"

"Yes, Sebbie?" came her mother's voice.

"May I have a word with you?"

"Of course, Dear. Come in."

Sebbie entered the room and saw that her mother was standing in front of the bureau, arranging her hair. "I'll be quiet." She tipped her head in the direction of the twins in the trundle bed.

Her mother nodded.

"I'd like to go to town with you," Sebbie whispered.

"Certainly," her mother whispered back. "I'll be happy for you to come along. I'll ask Bertie to stay in your stead and watch the twins and help Kit."

"I hope she won't be too disappointed—"

"I'm sure she won't mind." Her mother smiled. "Just this once."

"I suppose you're wondering why I want to go?"

"The thought did cross my mind." She looked at Sebbie through the mirror as she pushed hairpins into her upswept chignon. "You rarely go with me."

"I have a special mission to accomplish today. But first, I must ask your permission."

More question marks filled her mother's eyes. "Why don't we go to the kitchen?" She looked over at the twins, who were stirring in their sleep.

Within minutes, Sebbie and her mother were seated at the kitchen table, Sebbie telling her mother about the Bible verse she'd read the night before and her prayer for wisdom. She related the unusual dream and then her idea of selling the silk to finance the farrier.

At the mention of the wedding silk, her mother stared out the window, as if she were deep in contemplation. Long moments passed by.

"I believe God answered my prayer," Sebbie said in the quiet stillness. "I believe He gave me wisdom."

Her mother patted her hand. "I'm sure of it, Dear."

&

Later that morning, Sebbie made her way down the planked sidewalk to Hayes's General Store. Folded into the quilt she carried was her wedding silk. As she walked, the thought of selling her treasure produced perplexing emotions in her heart.

Pain, because of the parting it would mean, so final, so forever.

Pleasure, because of the healing it would bring.

Puzzlement, because life never seemed to be simple.

As she entered the store, the clanking of the bell on the door reminded her that she must buy some butter creams for little Ophelia. It had taken promises of bringing back two pieces of the fine candy to dry her tears when she found out Sebbie intended to go to town today.

"I don't want to stay with Kit and Bertie," Ophelia had wailed, stomping her foot. "I want Sebbie to keep us."

Now, as Sebbie made her way toward the long counter that held sundry items and a big hopper that ground coffee beans all day long at the customers' behest, she clutched the quilt tightly.

"Good morning, Sebbie," said Mr. Hayes, the owner of the general store. "Haven't seen you in a month of Sundays."

She smiled, dipped her chin. "Good morning to you, Sir. I usually stay home and keep the twins."

"Well, you need to bring them in sometime. Especially since Christmastime is fast coming upon us. That little Ophelia is. . .well, she wants her way, doesn't she? But she's a cutie. And Cecilia, well, she's a charmer."

"We call them our girlies."

He smiled. "What can I do for you this fine sunny day?"

She made furtive glances one way, then another, glad to see the store free of customers. "I wish to sell this." She unwrapped the quilt, drew out her prize, and placed it on the counter. "It's high-quality silk. Yards and yards of it. It was made in England, Mr. Hayes."

He ran his hand over the top fold, and she envisioned what it felt like, anticipated his response. "Mighty fine fabric," he said. "Mighty fine."

"I think it's worth a lot of money."

"I suppose so." He adjusted the little gold glasses that were perched on his nose and leaned closer to the fabric. "Wedding silk, I imagine?"

"Yes, Sir."

Again, he adjusted his glasses and peered into Sebbie's eyes. "You have any idea of its exact value?"

The wheels in Sebbie's brain turned with locomotive speed. She remembered the amount that Mr. Johnston, the farrier, had said he would need to treat Marco Polo when she and her mother stopped by to see him on their way to town.

Sebbie blurted out the sum.

"Sold." Mr. Hayes didn't even look at her, just drew out a sheet of brown paper, placed the silk in the center, folded it up like a present, and slid it under the counter.

"Thank you, Mr. Hayes. Someday, some lady will wear it proudly as she walks down the aisle."

He didn't respond, just handed her the amount she named.

She took the money, tucked it in her reticule, thanked him again profusely, and made her way to the door. Two ladies were entering as she approached, Mrs. Boutwell, the banker's wife, and her daughter, Verena Boutwell.

"Good morning, Sebbie," Mrs. Boutwell said.

"Good morning, Mrs. Boutwell and Verena," Sebbie responded, but her mind was far away, in a stall, beside a horse, an animal seventeen hands tall and as beautiful as ever a horse was.

In her mind's eye, she saw the spirited creature galloping at full speed across the field. She envisioned his powerful body, thought about his gallant spirit. He was reasonable and intelligent, bold and fearless, yet friendly and affectionate.

He was a beast of God.

He was a loved horse.

A mighty sick horse.

A horse that would soon be well.

twelve

Sebbie sat beside her mother on the buckboard, the wagon lumbering along the pockmarked way. The presence of Mr. Johnston trotting along behind them brought hope to Sebbie's heart. Soon, Marco Polo would be on his way to health, she was sure, and all would be well.

When they arrived home, she and her mother accompanied the farrier to the barn, followed by Kit—who was still getting around slower than her usual pace—and Bertie. The twins were content to make mud pies beside the porch steps.

As Mr. Johnston stepped into the stall, Marco Polo's ears flattened, and he whickered angrily, as he had been doing for days. Sebbie knew it was from his pain; and again, she was overcome with sorrow for the poor animal's plight.

"Let's have a look," Mr. Johnston said. He ran his hand down Marco Polo's leg, reaching for the foot. "Pick up," he commanded.

Marco Polo angrily whickered again, turned, and gave Mr. Johnston a glancing blow on his forearm.

"Yeow," he shouted. "His foot may be sore, but he can sure kick with it."

"He did that to me too," Bertie said. "Yesterday. When I was trying to soak his foot."

Mr. Johnston tried the pick-up signal once more. Once again, Marco Polo kicked him, then tried biting him. Mr. Johnston made a quick maneuver and grabbed the hoof firmly. Marco Polo made a move to pull away, but Mr. Johnston hung on, his firm, practiced hands grasping the hoof. Marco Polo finally submitted as he stood on three legs, motionless.

All the while Mr. Johnston worked on Marco Polo, he talked to him, telling him exactly what he was doing, letting him know why he was doing these things.

He removed the shoe, poked around, explained to Marco Polo that an abscess had formed, said that the only cure was to pare down the horn and evacuate the pus. He said that sometimes a horse had to be put down if the abscess was severe.

"What I'm going to do next, Marco Polo, will hurt for a moment," Mr. Johnston said, "but then it'll begin to feel better immediately. And then, in three- to five-days' time, old boy, you'll be back out in the field, prancing and parading in the pasture to your heart's content."

With a sharp knife and firm, sure strokes, Mr. Johnston cut away the horn, then punctured the abscess with the tip. He dabbed at it with a rag, applied some ointment to the frog and sole, finished his work, and in short order was backing out of the stall, giving Marco Polo an apple—a whole one—and telling him good-bye and God bless.

"Marco Polo, you'll be as fit as a fiddle in no time at all," he said.

As Mr. Johnston scrubbed his hands in a basin in the barn, Sebbie and her mother and sisters looking on, he told the Hanfords it was the worst abscess he had ever seen in all his years of tending to animals.

"He'll soon be sound," he said, a smile on his weathered face. "But if that abscess hadn't been treated, well. . ."

"I understand," Mama cut in.

"Yes." Sebbie bit her lip. Then relief flooded her, and she let out a satisfied sigh. "You saved him, Mr. Johnston. Thank you for what you did. I still can't get over it."

He mumbled a thanks, gave them instructions on the proper care and handling of the horse, and was quickly on his way.

As Sebbie and her mother sauntered back to the house to

see to supper, her mother stopped short. She picked up Sebbie's hands and faced her, looking intently into her eyes.

"You're the one who really saved him, Sebbie. Thank you for what you did. . .your wedding silk and all. I still can't get over it."

&

Dear Mr. Parks. . .

Sebbie looked up from the letter she had started, feeling like a bird out of prison. A week had passed, and just as Mr. Johnston had predicted, Marco Polo—how had he said it?—was prancing and parading in the pasture.

Kit was too. Of course neither of them were up to their previous speed, but they were out and about and almost back to their old selves.

"Thank You, Lord."

Kit had even taken to calf roping—at least pretend calf roping. High atop Marco Polo, she would throw out the rope, lassoing imaginary calves, then haul them in and throw out the rope again and again. The first time Sebbie saw her do it, it brought back a host of memories of branding time at Happy Acres.

Sebbie smiled, picked up her pen, and began writing. She told Mr. Parks the whole story of Marco Polo and his troubles, how they discovered his lameness, how they thought they had him on the road to mending what with the salve and soaking treatments and all, how dismayed they were when he hadn't responded, only grew worse, and how they had to call a farrier.

She continued writing, telling him in detail what Mr. Johnston did, how he cut out the abscess, how Marco Polo was now sound and whole and well, galloping across the pasture like nothing had ever been wrong.

She apologized for not writing about Marco Polo's plight when it was going on, told him how she had agonized over her decision to keep it from him, hoping against hope that Marco Polo would get better.

Thankfully, she wrote, he did get better and all was well.

&

Dear Mr. Parks,

You will probably be surprised when you receive this, but I felt compelled to write you. You see, I can't get over what has happened here at Happy Acres. I know Sebbie has already written you about Marco Polo, about his troubles and then his complete recovery. But there's more to the story than she would ever tell, and I feel I must inform you.

On the day Sebbie was born, my mother ordered a length of silk from England for Sebbie to be made into a wedding gown when the day came. It was very costly, but more than that, it had sentimental value that cannot be estimated.

Why am I telling you about Sebbie's wedding silk? Because she gave it up for you. She sold it to pay for the farrier's visit, and by doing so, she saved Marco Polo's life. She would never tell you this. But I felt you should know. I want to make sure you understand her commitment to Marco Polo. Though she's tender, she has a toughness to her that sometimes surprises even me.

With sincerity,
Mrs. Hanford

Griffin felt like the breath was knocked out of him when he read Mrs. Hanford's letter, so thrilled was he. Sebbie would do this for him? Give up her wedding silk from England? A gift from her long-dead grandmother, the woman she was named after? What a sacrifice. The girl was a treasure. What a prize he'd found in Miss Sebbie Hanford. She was a delight in every way.

He thought of how lovely she was, how beautiful. But she was more, much more. She was strong and courageous, sweet but spirited. He couldn't quit singing her praises. And she had a compliant attitude. That, coupled with her tender heart. . .well, thoughts of her made his own heart seem to melt.

Her sacrifice showed him just how tender she was. She had given up her greatest treasure in all the world, her irreplaceable wedding silk.

For him.

"Veritas praevalebit," he had told her when he left. "Truth has prevailed," he said emphatically.

He couldn't wait to get to Florida and take her in his arms and proclaim his love and ask for her hand in marriage. Of course, he would go gently, let protocol reign. He wouldn't be rash or crude. But he looked forward to the day when he would claim her as his own.

As his wife.

"Lord, I don't want just any wife," he had prayed a year ago, "but the wife Thou hast prepared for me."

He was as sure as the sun at noonday that Miss Sebbie Hanford was the wife the Lord had prepared.

"Thank You, Lord."

thirteen

Griffin finally arrived in Florida the last week of November. Just as he planned, he rented a room in the boardinghouse. The next thing he did was hire a horse and head out to Happy Acres.

Riding along, he was thankful for Florida's mild weather. Up north, it was sleeting and snowing. Here, though there was a slight chill in the air, the weather was refreshing, and the bright November sun shone like summer rays.

He sang, an old cowhand tune he had learned on the trail:

> " 'Cowboy's come a-courting,
> Cowboy's come to call.
> With a heart so true,
> I'll get a girl named Lou,
> Then I'll marry my sweet doll.' "

He threw his head back and chuckled as he trotted along. "Correction. Make that a girl named Sebbie."

That's what he had come to refer to her in his heart—Sebbie. Not Miss Hanford, the formal way of referring to a young woman, the one etiquette demanded, but her given name.

"One day—soon—I'll be courting you, Sebbie." The thought thrilled him.

Three-quarters of an hour later, he rode up to the Hanfords' house. Seeing no activity, he wondered. It was midmorning, and he thought he would at least hear the twins' clatter—well, little Miss Ophelia's anyhow—yet he neither saw nor heard anything, save for the birds singing in the towering oak tree to the side of the house. In fact, every branch appeared to be covered with birds, as if all the winged creatures in the North on their winter flight to the South had landed in the Hanfords' tree. It was a cacophony of sound, as pleasant as the orchestra he had heard last week in Philadelphia.

"Hello?" he called as he swung down from the saddle and tied his rented horse up at the post. "Anybody home?"

He thought he heard a childish squeal, walked around to the back of the house, and saw a sight that deeply moved him. Sebbie was bent over a giant black cauldron, her mother to her side. Beneath it was a hot fire, and inside the pot, apparently, was the family's wash.

With a long stick, Sebbie poked at laundry in the pot, picked up a piece, and flung it into another black cauldron beside the first one. Her mother swished it around, then pulled it out and handed it, dripping wet, to Miss Kit and Miss Bertie. They wrung it between them, carefully letting the water drip back into the pot and not on the ground. The well was quite a ways off, he knew.

They were so hard at work that they weren't even aware of his presence. He stood off at a distance, watching them. One day, as his plans progressed and blossomed, these wonderful women wouldn't have to do this dirty work. They would live as the ladies that they were, in his house, surrounded by fine furnishings and wearing frilly apparel, entertaining their friends in style. He would pamper them and protect them, and the thought brought him pleasure.

But seeing them this way, he was in anguish of soul, saddened at their straitened circumstances.

"Mr. Parks," little Miss Ophelia shrieked.

"Mr. Pawks," little Miss Cecilia said daintily.

"Mr. Parks," Miss Bertie yelled, dropping her end of the garment she was wringing so she could run toward him.

"Mr. Parks," Miss Kit squealed, tossing the garment back into the rinse pot and dashing across the yard.

When all four girls reached him, they greeted him exuberantly, and he was thrilled at their reception. The girlies begged him to swing them in the air, just as they had the day he left Happy Acres; and he complied, twirling them around and around. Miss Kit and Miss Bertie got in on the action, giving him hearty handshakes and calling out overzealous welcomes.

Mrs. Hanford approached. "Good morning, Mr. Parks. Welcome back to Happy Acres." She extended her hand in greeting.

He shook her hand, released it, and stepped back a gentlemanly distance. "Thank you, Mrs. Hanford. I hope I'm not coming at a bad time. I'm interrupting. . ." He tipped his head toward the cauldrons. "Your work."

"Nonsense, Mr. Parks. Friends are always welcome here."

Sebbie approached, dawdling across the yard it seemed to him—not coming joyously like he desired—and she looked flustered. She was rolling down the sleeves of her threadbare dress and hurriedly buttoning them at the wrists. She ran her hands along the sides of her hair and retied the apron strings at the small of her back.

He touched his black string tie and felt flustered himself, knew with a surety that she was embarrassed at her appearance. Inwardly, he scolded himself for not giving them warning, for not apprising them of his projected arrival time. What a lout he was. And here, he had wanted to make a good impression when he saw her after his long absence and the heartwarming letters they had exchanged. He had grand plans for Sebbie's future, as well as for her family's; and now, he was starting off on the wrong footing.

As she came near, she looked up at him, her familiar dazzling smile lighting her face. The sun danced on the gold in her hair, and her blue eyes matched his mother's aquamarine earrings and necklaces.

"Miss Hanford. . ." He was at a loss for words.

"Mr. Parks. . ." Apparently, she was too.

Little Miss Ophelia tugged on his coattail, asking him to swing her in the air again. Miss Kit and Miss Bertie started in about Marco Polo's antics, begging him to come to the barn right now. Miss Kit said she had learned cattle roping on Marco Polo, and Miss Bertie told him how much she loved Marco Polo and how hard it was going to be to part with the fine stallion.

"Girls," Mrs. Hanford said in a mildly reprimanding voice. "Please give Mr. Parks time to catch his breath. He's come all the way from town, and he needs some refreshment. Bertie, get him some water. Kit, see to his horse. Ophelia, Cecilia, there'll be time for you girlies later, I'm sure. Come, Mr. Parks, let us go inside."

At Mrs. Hanford's instructions, all moved quickly, doing as she said. She came up beside him and gestured toward the house.

He turned and looked at Sebbie.

"I–I'll be in momentarily, Mama." She didn't look at him, didn't even address him.

"Come, Mr. Parks." Mrs. Hanford awaited him.

He fell into step beside her as they walked down the raked path, though he would've preferred to stay with Sebbie, to converse with her and her alone. But there would be time for that later, he told himself.

Right now, he must honor Mrs. Hanford's wishes. After all, she was the one who would grant him permission to court Sebbie. She was the key to seeing the fulfillment of his plans.

"I trust all is well with you and your family, Mrs. Hanford."

"All is well, Mr. Parks."

"I cannot adequately express my deep gratitude for your allowing Marco Polo to board at Happy Acres during my absence. And for what Miss Hanford did. I don't take it lightly, the great favors you all have done me, particularly Sebbie. To show my thanks in only a small way, I've brought some things from town, though I intend to deal generously with Sebbie in my payment for her labors."

By then they were at the front of the house. They stopped near his rented horse, and he reached for a burlap sack tied onto the saddle horn. "A few foodstuffs. And some treats for the girlies."

"Why, Mr. Parks, this isn't necessary. The payment you and Sebbie agreed upon is more than generous."

"I wanted to do something extra. I hope you are aware of how special your family has become to me."

"Yes." Mrs. Hanford's voice was as quiet as a mouse. She said no more, just looked down at the ground, not even making an attempt to look in the sack as he expected.

He wondered at her lack of words. She was the epitome of good breeding, a gifted conversationalist. Perhaps he had insulted her with the foodstuffs. He chided himself for the second time that day. First, he had embarrassed Sebbie. Now, he had offended her mother. He wished he could undo all he had done and start over, fresh. But his intentions were pure. Surely, she knew this.

"Won't you stay for dinner?" she finally said, gesturing at the porch steps, and they climbed them together.

"You're sure? Then, yes, I'd be delighted to accept your gracious offer." One more inward scolding. *You're too eager, Pardner.* But he couldn't help himself. If only Mrs. Hanford knew, if only Sebbie knew, what course he had charted for them, they would. . .they would be in a transport of delight. But he reminded himself that he must go slowly, proceed cautiously.

These are gentlewomen, he told himself, *and they must be dealt with in such manner.*

❦

All through dinner, Sebbie hardly said a word. She felt like the weight of the world rested on her shoulders. Her emotions were at the bursting point. She wanted to please her mother. But she wanted to. . .what did she want concerning Mr. Parks? Ah, she knew for certain. She wanted to receive his attentions. She was sure that's what he had in mind, giving her his attentions. She wanted to receive them warmly, to embrace them, to embrace him. . . .

She blushed, then mentally shook herself as she passed him the peas. Her emotions were going off in all directions. She glanced at him, then averted her eyes as she took a small bite of potatoes from her plate. He was all lightness and jest, especially with Kit and Bertie and the girlies, just as he had been the first night he came to Happy Acres. She would never forget that evening as long as she lived, when they had sung together, and he'd regaled them with funny stories and tall tales. He exemplified all the virtues she could want in a man.

The potatoes seemed to stick in her throat, and she swallowed deeply. Her eyes misted as confusing thoughts swirled in her mind.

Yes, he's all my heart could desire. But he's not what my mother desires for me.

The thought hit her with dark foreboding. *And I must honor my mother.* That had always brought pleasure to Sebbie. It was her manner of living, of thinking, of doing, of being— to obey her mother in all things. But it didn't bring pleasure to her now. It only brought pain of the worst sort.

She looked at Mr. Parks once more as he told a story about a happening in Philadelphia last month, every eye at the table focused on him, even Ophelia quiet and absorbed for the moment.

"Obey your parents in the Lord," the Holy Writ exhorted. In all ways, at all times, that had been the way she operated.

And that would be the way she operated right now, what she would put into practice, what she would carry into execution.

❧

All the way back to town, Griffin was puzzled. And hurt. He'd expected to find in Sebbie a warm heart. All he found was a cold shoulder.

Musings of the debutante in Philadelphia, the brass-hearted Miss Hearst who had tried to trick him, floated through his brain, but he refused to let them stay there. They had no bearing on this situation, no bearing at all.

What was the matter with Sebbie? All through dinner, she had hardly spoken a word. Afterward, in the barn, when he was saddling Marco Polo, she had said not a sentence. Of course, her sisters were ganged around, chattering like magpies, telling him this and that.

And he had been so excited about seeing Marco Polo. He had wanted to know every detail of Marco Polo's trouble, his treatment, and his prognosis. Was that the reason Sebbie was so quiet? Because she couldn't get a word in edgewise?

Had she been evasive and standoffish because. . .because she wasn't interested in him?

If that were true, it would be a hard blow to endure.

But he shook off the dark thought. He had to fathom this out, let reason be his guide. He would not jump to conclusions.

"Giddyap, Boy." Was the care of Marco Polo too much for her? Did she resent the heavy responsibility Marco Polo had become, what with his hoof trouble, and then the worry and fretting over him, as she expressed in her letter? Though he felt bad at what she had gone through, he had no way of knowing that these events would transpire when he had asked her to board Marco Polo. He had no way of knowing that Marco Polo would become a burden to her.

Why? Why? Why?

The word pounded his brain repeatedly, giving him an ache in the head. He rubbed his temples.

Somehow, someway, he would find the answer to this mystery. He was determined to win the hand of Miss Sebbie Hanford.

fourteen

Two days later, Griffin bounded down the steps at the boardinghouse, intent on getting to the bank to take care of business. He was pleasantly surprised to see Mrs. Hanford standing near the bottom of the stairs, her quilts displayed behind her on a table in the bend of the staircase.

"Mrs. Hanford, I'm pleasured to see you," he said.

"Hello, Mr. Parks."

"This will save me a trip to Happy Acres, though I would relish it. As I've said before, there's happiness at Happy Acres."

She didn't say anything, but question marks loomed in her eyes.

He stopped on the last step and grasped the newel post. He chided himself. He shouldn't have said that about happiness at Happy Acres. He was being too forward. He needed to go gently. "What I mean, is, I need to talk with you about a matter. I have something to ask of you. I intended to ride out to see you this very afternoon."

She leaned over the table and straightened the corner of a red-and-white quilt.

He took a step toward her. Was she purposely ignoring him? Whatever for? She had been so hospitable at Happy Acres. Never mind trying to fathom this out. He had been doing that a lot lately, trying to make sense of everything including Sebbie's actions—or lack of actions, he should say.

With a shrug of his shoulders, he decided he would plunge in and ask away. "I've become aware that there's a town social this Friday night, following Thanksgiving. I assume you are aware of this, Mrs. Hanford?"

"Yes."

"Are you going?"

"No."

He was surprised. From what he had heard, there weren't many occasions like that in this town. If you could even call it a town, it was so small. Still, most people would welcome a party, a diversion from the starkness of life. Why wasn't she going? "What about your daughters?"

"Kit and Bertie are too young for a grown-up party. They'll get their turn for frivolity at the school recitation party at Christmastime. The girlies too."

"But Sebbie's going to the town social, surely."

"Yes, Sebbie is attending."

He was cheered. "May I accompany her? If that is her desire, of course?"

"She is attending the social, as I said. But she's being escorted by someone else."

Griffin drew in a ragged breath. "May I ask by whom?"

"The young Mr. Artemis Boutwell." She had a proud look in her eyes.

He reeled, then steadied himself at the newel post. "I see." He was so stunned that at first he could not respond adequately. Never in a thousand years had he expected this. All the while he was writing Sebbie—and falling in love with her—he thought it would be a simple thing to woo her and to win her. He would treat her with affection, shower attention on her. She would fall in love with him, they would become betrothed, and then they would make wedding arrangements. It was as simple as that. He bit his bottom lip. He couldn't believe this new turn of events. A rival.

"Mr. Boutwell made several overtures to Sebbie this past year. When he extended the invitation to the social, she. . .she gladly accepted."

Griffin wondered why. What was the cause of Sebbie's

suddenly accepting this man's attentions?

"Mr. Boutwell's father owns the bank." Mrs. Hanford thrust her chin high in the air.

"I see," he said again, for lack of anything better, though he did indeed see. At least he thought he did, and he could've said plenty more. A question pounded at his heart. Was it Sebbie's desire to be with Mr. Boutwell? Or her mother's?

"Do you know Mr. Boutwell, Mr. Parks?"

"I know his father. I was headed to see him just now. I–I. . .well, I must be hurrying along." He felt like the fool that he was. "I trust you have a good day, Mrs. Hanford." She certainly needed to make sales.

"I trust so too, Mr. Parks."

He dipped his chin. "Good-bye." He was at a loss for words again, so unlike him. "Godspeed," he finally said.

"Same to you." Her tone was clipped.

As he made his way across the lobby and then out the door, he fought feelings of anger. On he went, walking briskly toward the bank, remembering the day little Miss Ophelia had shown him Sebbie's wedding silk in the polished cedar chest.

"I heard Mama tell Sebbie that as soon as she finds a rich man, we're going to have a wedding around here," the tyke had said.

He recalled how, just moments before little Miss Ophelia had come in the room, he had been thinking affectionately of Sebbie. Then, when the tyke made her announcement, he had been crushed.

Later, as he watched Sebbie milking the cow, he shaped his plan concerning her. He would write her and get to know her so she could prove herself. And then he would come to Florida and board in town for awhile so he could observe her and scrutinize her motives.

He would put her through a sort of test or experiment. *Experimentum crucis.*

As he had mapped out, everything had gone by the card, and their correspondence had commenced. Indeed, he had gotten to know Sebbie. Not only that, he had fallen in love with her.

He thought of the day God had dealt with him about his judgmental attitude. The Bible verse about man looking on the outward appearance not the heart had greatly impacted him, and he realized that was exactly what he was doing with Sebbie. He had repented to the Lord and then decided to lay aside his qualms and accept Sebbie at face value, for who she was. And in his heart, he had come to know that her intentions were pure.

Now, though, she had rebuffed him; and not only that, she was pursuing a relationship with the banker's son.

He smirked, so grim did he feel. This morning, her mother had purred about the banker's son escorting Sebbie. That could only mean one thing. It proved the reality of what little Miss Ophelia had repeated to him, about her mama looking for a rich man for Sebbie. All Mrs. Hanford wanted was a wealthy man for her daughter. That smacked of deceit. And apparently, she would go to any lengths to get it.

Well, he would wash his hands of the whole thing.

He stopped in the middle of the walk. No, he would not, could not, give up Sebbie this easily. He would find a new strategy. There was another means of access. He just had to formulate it.

Oh, Lord, how will this work out? He had been so sure Sebbie was the one for him. What could he do about the situation? What could he say? He knew for a certainty he could not all of a sudden reveal that he too was a wealthy man. Not that he minded their knowing. In fact, he intended to tell them at some point. But if he did this now, it would make the whole affair indelicate; and he would not subject these ladies to indelicacy.

Perhaps if he—

"You've made too many plans, Son," the Lord seemed to whisper. *"Look to Me instead. Trust, and then obey."*

"Okay, Lord," he whispered as he walked on. "I'll try."

&

Late that afternoon, Griffin breezed through the boarding-house lobby, feeling squeamish about having to pass Mrs. Hanford. Obviously she wanted nothing to do with him; and being the gentleman that he was, he didn't want to subject her to something unwanted.

He eyed the lobby, saw that she was engaged in conversation with a customer, and with chin down, minding his own business, he made a beeline for the staircase.

"Mr. Parks?"

He looked up when he heard her voice, saw the customer standing nearby.

"May I have a word with you?"

He was surprised. Her tone was amicable, cordial even. "Certainly, Mrs. Hanford. At your wish."

"I'll only be a few moments longer."

"I'll wait to the side, then."

A quarter hour later, she approached him where he sat in a chair, and immediately he sprang to his feet.

"Mr. Parks, I–I. . ." She seemed to falter for words. "I want to offer a sincere apology."

"You've done nothing amiss."

"But I have."

"Come, Mrs. Hanford, let your mind be at peace—"

"It can't until I apologize."

He wondered. What would she say? What was she thinking?

"This morning, I was. . .I was. . ." She paused, looking

down at her hands, which were clenched in tight balls. She opened one, studied her fingers.

He felt bad for her, but there was nothing to say.

She looked up at him, her gaze never wavering. "This morning, I was indifferent. . .graceless. For that, I most humbly apologize. That's not my way."

"But—"

"Please, hear me out."

He nodded and leaned against the wall, being careful not to get too close to the gas sconce.

"At Happy Acres, things are. . ." She stared down at her fingers once again. Finally she looked up, and he noticed that her eyes were as blue as Sebbie's and just as sincere.

"Things have been difficult since. . .since my dear husband. . .passed on," she continued, her eyes misting over. Then she thrust back her shoulders, a resoluteness to her stance, her tears in check. "As I said this morning, Mr. Boutwell has long had a shine for Sebbie. Unfortunately. . ." She swallowed hard. "Unfortunately Sebbie has never returned his sentiments."

Relief flooded through him.

"Sebbie is a wonderful girl."

How well he knew.

"An obedient young woman—"

"A worthy and admired trait any mother would be proud of in her daughter," he said.

She nodded. "I–I thought Mr. Boutwell had given up on Sebbie. He has made no overture for quite some time. In all fairness to him, Sebbie deserved his shunning. But when he asked to take her to the social. . ." She smiled that same brilliant smile as Sebbie's. "Well, let's put it this way. Sebbie finally agreed to give him a chance. . .a chance to. . ." She lowered her voice. "To win her affections." Once more, a smile lit up her face.

Now Griffin was the one swallowing hard. As before, he was at a loss for words.

"This morning, when you asked permission to escort her, I was frightened."

Flabbergasted, he interjected, "Frightened, Mrs. Hanford? Of me?"

"Of what this could mean. . .to Sebbie. . .to us. . .your asking to escort her." She clutched at the lace on her collar. "I–I. . .what I'm trying to say is. . .what I'm asking of you, Mr. Parks, is. . .well, I'm asking you to steer clear of Sebbie. I'm asking you. . .not to muddle my. . .machinations."

Matchmaking, you mean.

"I have my reasons." She paused. "Do you catch my meaning, Mr. Parks?"

"I certainly do." He knew all about plans. He had made plenty of them. He knew how you went about your mental musings with precision detail, how you deep-laid them, how you carried out your machinations—as she called it—to the nth degree. He also knew how plans went awry. His certainly had.

But he would not be the cause of Mrs. Hanford's plans falling through. He would do as she bid. He would retreat, let this mother do what she thought best for her daughter, honor her intentions. He would show her the milk of human kindness, do as he would have her do to him.

And then, then, he would have to rely on God to work it all out.

That was the only way.

fifteen

The afternoon of the social, Sebbie took particular pains with her appearance. She wanted to look her very best. A social was a few-and-far-between event in this neck of the woods—Wit's End Corner her mother jestingly called it. Just getting to go to the gathering brought pleasure to her. The town was finally growing, enough to warrant a party like this. Perhaps there would be many more to come.

All day she had worn curlpapers in the front part of her hair, wanting a few curls to dot her face. Now, standing before the small mirror over her bureau, she took the papers off and combed the curls into place.

She thought about the reasons she was going to the social tonight.

The reason.

The only reason.

She was going at the behest of her mother. Her mother had been so enthusiastic about the social. It was as if she had become a girl again in the last few days as they sewed almost around the clock, remaking a dress of Mama's from her Massachusetts days.

All of this fanfare—the sewing, the curlpapers, the taking of pains to get ready—was for her mother's sake.

Yes, Sebbie would go and do as her mother said. She would give Mr. Boutwell a chance to win her affections. She shuddered. But then she rallied, throwing out her chest, taking a deep breath. If she could not give herself to Mr. Boutwell's attentions, well, at least she had tried. And she would have a pleasant time tonight enjoying the fine company of other young people.

She looked across the minuscule bedroom, saw her mother's made-over blue silk gown draped across the bed. For a moment, a secret longing for elegant attire threatened to overtake her. But she knew such a thing wasn't possible, and she didn't lament long. There was simply no use.

She crossed the room, picked up the gown, pulled it over her head, then heard the door open and close, heard her mother's voice.

"Need any help, Dear?"

"Yes, thank you, Mama." She wiggled into the light blue silk, hoping it wouldn't muss her hair too badly, smoothing it down at her waist and wrists. "Will you button me up?"

"Certainly." Her mother came around behind her and began fastening the long row of buttons up Sebbie's back. "How I wish you had something really fitting to wear tonight. Though you look like a flower. Your sweetness of heart and soul blooms in your face."

"Why, thank you, Mama. What beautiful words."

"Not as beautiful as you are, Sebbie. But as I said earlier, I do wish you had something really fitting to wear."

"This is fitting." Sebbie smoothed the silk, then touched the tatting at her throat, something she herself had fashioned and sewn on. She tucked into her collar a posy of pink camellias she had picked not an hour ago. The bush near the porch was in full bloom—prairie flowers her mother called them—and she thought the blossoms were as beautiful as a queen's jewels.

"If only. . ." A sad wistfulness clouded her mother's eyes.

"Don't fret, Mama."

"Oh, the gowns and frocks I had as a girl." Mama stopped her buttoning, came around in front of Sebbie, and sank to the bed seemingly in deep thought. "The night I met your papa, I was wearing a maroon-colored gown with a matching velvet headdress." She brushed at her graying hair. "It came complete with feathers—the height of fashion in those days. The skirt," she explained, touching the front of her cotton apron, "was ornamented with maroon glacé, and the collar was of Irish point." She ran her hands down her arms. "The sleeves. . .the sleeves were magnificent. I designed them myself and told the seamstress exactly what I had in mind. They were like the ones in the portrait of Marguerite de Valois, the puffs and frills separated by bands of maroon velvet like the headdress. At my throat was my mother's strand of pearls."

"Ah, Mama, it sounds magnificent."

"It was. Truly." Sebbie's mother sighed. "Your only ornament is three pink flowers in the collar of a twenty-five-year-old, made-over gown." She let out another heavy sigh. "Sebbie, what you've missed. . .what all you girls have missed. . ."

"I'm going to miss Mr. Boutwell's ride to town because I won't be ready, Mama. He'll have to leave without me." She laughed. "Please. Finish buttoning me up, and stop this talk about wanting me to have fitting apparel. I feel like a princess." She pirouetted; and as her skirts swirled about her, she backed toward her mother, who was still sitting on the bed.

The door burst open, and in ran Kit and Bertie shrieking and laughing, as happy as could be, as if they too were going to the social.

Sebbie noticed Bertie shut the door firmly behind her.

"Look at you," Kit squealed as she tugged on one of Sebbie's curls, "a-primping and a-prinking."

"Ouch," Sebbie cried. "Do that again, and I'll strike you from my list of people I'm going to bring a party dainty to."

Kit fell on her knees, mockingly contrite. Then she jumped up and hugged Sebbie fiercely. "Hallelujah, Sebbie's going to a social."

"You'll crumple her gown," Bertie called out. "Take care, Kit." But she hugged Sebbie too, as strenuously as Kit had done.

"That's all right," Sebbie said. "I like hug crumples."

"Sebbie," Bertie said. "Mr. Boutwell is here."

Sebbie nearly jumped out of her skin. "Already? Thank the Lord you shut the door behind you, Bertie. Otherwise, he might've heard your foolishness."

Bertie beamed. "I'm already envisioning a man coming to call on me. That's why I thought to shut the door. I want everything to be perfect when that day arrives."

Sebbie smoothed the folds of her gown. She picked at the tatting on her collar, fingered the camellias tucked inside it. She fiddled with her chignon. That's why her mother wished for Sebbie to marry well, so she could give the girls and girlies a chance at the good things in life. What a responsibility that was to Sebbie, so heavy it was almost like a rock weighing down on her.

As fast as Kit and Bertie breezed in the door, they breezed out, calling over their shoulders for Sebbie to hurry, that Mr. Boutwell was waiting.

"I do hope you will try and like Mr. Boutwell," her mother whispered as soon as the door was fast shut. She fluffed Sebbie's skirts, then handed her a delicate, crocheted shawl. "He is a fine young man, deserving of your endearments." She talked on of plighted troths, sweet matrimony, and lasting love; and Sebbie felt her face growing warm.

On and on, her mother continued her comments, in low tones of course; but Sebbie's mind was far away, on letters filled with endearments, letters from Mr. Griffin Parks. . .her Griffin.

She banished the thought as quickly as it jangled through her mind. She must not even think of Griffin.

Not now.

Not tonight.

Not ever.

❧

Griffin was the first person Sebbie did think of that evening, because he was the first person she saw. As soon as she entered the white clapboard building with Mr. Boutwell at her elbow, there, across the room, leaning against the wall and talking to the senior Mr. Boutwell, was Griffin. When she made eye contact with him, she wondered if she blushed. She was thinking about her private use of his given name. Griffin.

She would have to relinquish that little habit, pleasurable though it was. She knew it wasn't right. She must give her full attention to the man at her side, Mr. Artemis Boutwell, as she had promised her mother.

The young Mr. Artemis Boutwell, as everyone referred to him, was tall like Griffin—no, Mr. Parks. She must remember to refer to him by his surname from now on. Mr. Boutwell was nearly as handsome too. Sebbie couldn't fault his appearance. His apparel had always been clean and pressed on the various occasions when Sebbie met him. Tonight, he wore a gray suit coat and black trousers. With his crisp white shirt and striped satin tie, he looked dashing, as Bertie would say. His brown hair was combed neatly. But what bothered her was how hollow his eyes looked, so vacant, almost like there was no feeling in them.

A quick glance in Mr. Parks's direction showed her that he was just as nicely dressed and groomed as young Mr. Boutwell. He wore a dark blue suit and a light blue shirt with a black string tie. He looked dashing too. But when their gazes locked momentarily, she was reminded of just how much feeling was in his expression. Too much. She quickly averted her eyes.

All through the evening, thankfully, she managed to avoid Mr. Parks. Actually, it wasn't hard. He seemed to be avoiding her. That was good. But why? Before, on every occasion she had seen him, he had sought her out and tried to draw her into conversation. But not tonight. He stayed on one side of the room, she on the other.

During refreshment time, which followed lively games and

a square dance of a sort, Sebbie sat talking with Mr. Boutwell's sister, Verena, who seemed overly solicitous.

They talked—mostly Verena—of fabrics for gowns and new styles in footwear and the winter visitors streaming in from the North and a host of other trivial things.

Sebbie couldn't help but think of the twins' patched frocks and the nearly empty canisters and other somber realities facing the Hanfords. They were sorely pressed, reduced to dire straits.

Would she be able to change all that? She stole a peek at Mr. Boutwell where he stood near several men guffawing loudly, playfully poking one man in the midsection, himself being poked in return. Apparently they were joking and teasing as gentlemen sometimes did.

She took a small bite of lemon pie and chewed slowly. If she gave Mr. Boutwell any attention at all, any flattery in the least, she was sure he would come courting, and then she could wrangle a proposal out of him. But would that be honest? Perhaps she could learn to love him. That would make it right, wouldn't it? What about arranged marriages? Didn't couples learn to love after they were already chosen for each other? Couples in India or some other country she had read about? And certainly couples in the Bible?

"It's just as easy to fall in love with a rich man as it is a poor one," her mother always said.

Until now, Sebbie had always laughed when her mother said that. Tonight, she felt like crying. It hit too close to home.

"I'm on the lookout for the perfect fabric for my wedding gown," Verena was saying. "I want to be ready when the big day comes. I'd like it to be silk. Or satin, if it's fine enough."

Sebbie thought of a length of beautiful fabric sitting in a brown paper wrapper under Mr. Hayes's counter. She envisioned its shimmery folds, could almost feel its smooth softness as she rubbed her fingers together in thin air.

"Sebbie?" Verena asked.

Knowing she would never wear her beloved wedding silk ordered from England by her late grandmother on the day Sebbie was born, she fought back a tear.

"Sebbie? Is anything the matter?"

"No, no, of course not." At that moment, Sebbie caught Mr. Parks's gaze on her, and she didn't know what to think.

Long moments passed as she and Verena ate the party dainties, conversing more, Verena mostly, as before, about a myriad of subjects.

Verena jumped to her feet. "Come with me, Sebbie."

Sebbie wasn't finished with her pie. She had at least three more bites. "Where to?"

"I need more lemonade." Verena held up her cup. "I'm fresh out. Come with me. Please?"

Why did Verena need her to go along to the refreshment table? It was a simple matter of refilling her cup. But she decided not to question her. Instead, she stood and followed her. Within moments, they were standing at the table, Verena ladling lemonade into her cup.

"Would you like some more, Sebbie?"

"Mine's still full."

"Mine's full too." Verena held up her cup, then gestured to some chairs near the table. "Why don't we sit on this side of the room for now?"

"But the other side suits me fine. And besides, it's not nearly as crowded over there." Sebbie pulled at her collar to let air get down her neck, being careful to keep a firm hold on the three camellias. "So many people in here has made it a little warm."

"But this side is more to my liking." Verena tipped her head in the direction across the room to where they had been sitting.

Sebbie followed Verena's gaze and saw two young women, one a girl really, sitting next to the seats she and Verena had just vacated. She could see that the two women were not appropriately dressed for a social. Their apparel looked nearly as bad as her workday clothing, their hair was unkempt, and their general appearance was untidy. Her heart went out to them.

Verena giggled. "We simply have to move, Sebbie. I wouldn't want us to get. . ." She whispered the word "bugs" in Sebbie's ear.

Sebbie made no show of her disgust. But inside, she wanted to cringe. Here was Verena Boutwell, supposedly in high cotton, yet in reality she was as crass as a crude clown. And not only crass, but. . .but prejudiced and unkind and rude, and she could think of a host of other adjectives to describe her.

The young Mr. Boutwell approached, waving a small slip of paper. "Sebbie, I drew your name for the promenade."

"You did?" She was surprised. That was a long shot.

"Yes." He offered her his elbow. "Ready to go?"

Sebbie knew this practice at parties. Promenades. The women wrote their names on slips of paper and dropped them in a hat. At a given time, the men took turns drawing out the slips. Then the couples promenaded around the perimeter of the property for fifteen minutes, supposedly for a romantic, sometimes-moonlit stroll. Occasionally the privacy of the promenades produced betrothals.

Mr. Boutwell kept his elbow extended. "Several couples have already started their proms, Miss Hanford. Let's join them."

The thought made her tremble. But she held her own. She must be polite and abide by social customs. Of course Mr. Boutwell would maintain proper protocol, but she desperately longed to avoid this required close contact with him. Putting her feelings aside, she smiled up at him. "Certainly, Mr. Boutwell. Let me get my shawl."

❧

Sebbie made her way to the cloak area, a secluded alcove

with hooks dotting the wall. As she reached for her shawl, she sighed. She was anxious to get home. She was tired. In body. And in company.

Oh, Mr. Boutwell had been the perfect escort. And he would do just as she expected during the promenade outside. He would be as gentlemanly as Mr. Parks had always been.

She caught herself. Would she never be able to think of any man without comparing him to Mr. Parks? That thought troubled her. How would a man get a fair turn from her? Mr. Parks was the paragon, in her estimation. He was perfect, in every area but one—at least according to her mother. He was only a cowhand.

"How are you finding the evening, Miss Hanford?"

She whirled around, and there, to her surprise, stood Mr. Parks, reaching for his jacket.

"I trust it's to your liking, Miss Hanford? I'm finding it most enjoyable."

She felt all fluttery inside at his nearness, couldn't seem to find her voice. Why couldn't things have been different? But it was no use to lament over what could never be. She grabbed a breath. "Yes, Mr. Parks. It is a pleasant evening."

"The music is lively."

She thought about the banjoes and the guitars and the harmonicas. "Yes."

"The refreshments are tasty."

She remembered the lemon pie and the caramel cake and the sugar cookies and the candies and the luscious lemonade. The pie and the lemonade had been made from citrus fruit picked in the area that very morning, she'd been told. "How right you are. Quite tasty."

"Are you looking forward to the promenade?"

Her face felt aflame. She knew she must be blushing scarlet. Avoiding his gaze, she smoothed the folds of her gown. She picked at the tatting on her collar and fingered the three pink camellias tucked in it. She fiddled with her chignon. Finally she drew on her shawl, stared down at its bow, tied it, untied it, and tied it again, wishing the floor would swallow her.

"There you are," the young Mr. Boutwell said, appearing from out of nowhere. "I was wondering what was keeping you." He glared at Mr. Parks.

"I was just asking Miss Hanford if she's looking forward to being your partner for the promenade." Mr. Parks's eyes lit up, his face one big smile. "The partner you said you'd move heaven and earth to get." He chuckled heartily.

Mr. Boutwell's glare grew colder, darker.

Sebbie wondered what was going on between the two.

"I'm waiting for her answer." Mr. Parks was smiling, his arms folded across his barrel chest.

"So, what about it, Miss Hanford?" Mr. Boutwell asked. "What do you think about our outdoor promenade? Yours and mine?"

She drew her shawl tightly about her, stared through the glass of a nearby window. "I think. . .I think it looks. . .rather chilly out."

ૐ

When Sebbie walked outside with Mr. Boutwell, she noticed several couples standing around talking, others strolling arm in arm. But it was hard to tell who was out and about. Save for a lantern hanging from the stair railing and a sliver of a moon above, it was dark.

Mr. Boutwell offered his arm, and they began to walk. He greeted a few people as they passed them, but he appeared to be deep in thought.

She tried to envision what it would be like to be joined matrimonially to him as they sauntered along. He was kind. He was nice-looking. He was prosperous. All were admirable attributes.

But for the life of her, she could not see them as husband

and wife. Oh, she was trying. She wanted to please her mother. Perhaps if she conversed with him more, got to know him better, then her sentiments could be turned favorably toward him. But she wasn't a conversationalist, like her mother was. Her mother's personality sparkled. Sebbie, on the other hand, was quiet, at times even shy. Still, Mr. Boutwell deserved her best efforts.

She gathered her inner resources. "It's a nice social, Mr. Boutwell."

"Yes, it is. The best."

"Thank you for inviting me."

"My pleasure. We are planning a few more in the near future." He paused. "I hope, Miss Hanford, that you will accompany me again. You will, won't you?"

She was stumped. Here she had made the decision to try and talk with him to get to know him better, and now he was asking her a question she found hard to answer.

"I am thrice happy in your company," he said.

"An old saying, Mr. Boutwell—"

"Which means—"

"A person is elated—"

"To be with the other one," he said, completing the saying and then joining Sebbie in laughter over their playful interruptions, a pleasant camaraderie springing up between them. That pleased her.

"My father used to say that to my mother," she said quietly, remembering.

"I'll say it again, Miss Hanford. I am thrice happy in your company."

She didn't respond, just continued walking by his side. He didn't say anything either. It was simply a pleasant togetherness in the silence as they strolled on, twigs breaking under their feet occasionally, muted voices of nearby couples wafting through the night air.

At last, he broke the quiet. "Is there anything you can think of, to add to the next social? To make it better than this one? I've been appointed to the committee."

"No. Not at the moment. But I'll give it some thought."

"Everything has been perfect, hasn't it?"

"Yes. Everything."

"Except for one thing."

"What's that?

"When those two women came in." He let out a slight hiss.

"Which two women?" She knew perfectly well which two women he was referring to. That's all Verena could talk about. Those two women. Verena was steeped in prejudice to the hilt. Apparently he was too.

"It's clear that those two women were out of their element tonight. Why, a person can tell by the looks of them how. . . how terribly out of place they are." He smirked, then proceeded to describe—with disdain—their clothing, their hairdos, their mannerisms. "People like that should understand their low station in life and not intrude in places where they shouldn't be."

She bristled. " 'People like that,' you said? In a low station of life? People like. . .like the Hanford family?"

"I–I. . ." He rubbed the back of his neck. "Forgive me. My comments were unkind. . .perhaps."

Her insides churned. " 'Perhaps'?" She was incredulous at his audacity.

"You don't seem to be like that, Miss Hanford. You're refined and genteel, even if you are. . .uh. . .ill-furnished. You're not uncouth like those. . .those brand of people are."

Her ire was getting the best of her. " 'Brand'?" she fired back, jerking her arm from the crook of his elbow. "And just what brand am I, Mr. Boutwell?" She stopped dead in her tracks and faced him.

"Come, Miss Hanford." He reached to tuck her hand back

in his elbow, but she resisted.

"Let's see, Mr. Boutwell. I'm ill-furnished, like them, due to the lack of funds—"

"You're taking this all wrong—"

"I'm orphaned, due to the lack of a father—"

"I never dreamed you would respond like this." He let out a snide huff.

She rattled off a few more things, not giving him a chance to interrupt. Finally she drew a deep breath. "But there's one thing I'm not, Mr. Boutwell."

"What's that?" he snapped.

"I'm not available."

"Is that right?"

"That's right. To your 'brand' anyway."

"Is there anything else you'd like to say?"

"Yes. I'd like to go home now."

sixteen

The following Sunday morning, Sebbie filed into the same white clapboard building where the social had been the Friday night before. Today, it was serving as a church. A circuit preacher would be speaking; and by the buzz of happy voices and pleasant expressions, it was evident that this was a special event in the people's lives.

Walking in front of Sebbie were her mother and the girlies and behind her Kit and Bertie. They made their way to their seats, Sebbie having to prod the girlies down the rows of chairs. They were more interested in seeing and talking to other children than in taking their places.

As Sebbie sat down and situated her skirts, she thought of the disastrous evening with Mr. Boutwell. She fanned herself with her handkerchief, recalling it, particularly the promenade. Where had she come up with her bravery? Spitfire was what Kit proudly called it when she heard of the incident. Sebbie only knew that she couldn't refrain from speaking her mind in the face of Mr. Boutwell's hateful remarks about the two women in dire straits.

From the corner of her eye, she saw Mr. Boutwell enter and find a seat across the aisle from her, and she fanned harder. Now she was embarrassed at her outburst at Mr. Boutwell. Then she was enraged at his bias. How dare the man treat another human being with such disdain and dislike?

The morning after the social when she had told her mother what happened, at first her mother seemed very concerned— for a couple of reasons, she told her.

"Sebbie," her mother had said, "will your outburst show a

lack of good breeding?" Then she added, "And will it mean the end of Mr. Boutwell's pursuit of you?"

Sebbie waited on tenterhooks as her mother seemed to ponder her next words.

"Your paroxysm of disgust showed excellent breeding as far as I'm concerned," her mother finally said, triumph in her tone. "Anyone knows that a true member of the gentility takes up for the unfortunate, rather than putting him down, and that's exactly what you did."

Her mother talked on. "Will Mr. Boutwell come round again? I think not. His pride will keep him away. But that's all right too, my dear. The Bible says, 'Pride goeth before destruction, and an haughty spirit before a fall.' We don't want any more falls around here, do we?" She smiled. "Besides, I'd rather not have my daughter associated with Mr. Boutwell's 'brand.'"

Her mother had hugged her then. "You did what I asked you to do. You gave your attentions to him with an open heart and mind. I want you to know how much I admire you. You've always been a meek, obedient daughter, and for that, I am grateful. The Bible says, 'Blessed are the meek: for they shall inherit the earth.' Sebbie, mark my words. Good things are going to come to you."

Waiting for the service to begin, Sebbie sighed. Thank the Lord her mother had been understanding about the incident with Mr. Boutwell. And not only that, her mother had said she admired Sebbie. That brought a glow to her spirit even now, thinking about it.

Sebbie glanced around and saw that the room was fast filling up. When she spotted Mr. Parks three rows behind her, her heart started its familiar fluttering, but she commanded it to be still. It could never be. Knowing he was behind her, feeling as if his eyes were staring holes in her back, she did what she always did when she had a case of nerves. She smoothed the folds of her dark blue dress. She picked at the lace on her collar and fingered the three pink camellias stuck in it. She fiddled with her chignon.

Then she stilled her busy hands, willing herself not to think about Mr. Parks. But it was hard, knowing he was so near yet so far away. Putting her mind to more constructive use, she gave her full attention to the preacher and his sermon.

"Let us turn to Matthew 5:5," the preacher intoned. "Brother and sisters, listen as I read. 'Blessed are the meek—'"

Sebbie didn't hear another word of the verse, just glanced at her mother. Mama gave her a knowing nod, and Sebbie blinked back a tear. How fitting that the Lord would anoint His servant to preach from the very text that had held so much meaning for her lately.

For long minutes, the circuit preacher ministered eloquently on the verse from the Beatitudes. "Blessed are the meek: for they shall inherit the earth."

"Folks, meekness does not mean weakness. It means strength made tender. It means having grit, but wrapping it up with grace. It means being strong enough to do what's right and having wisdom to know how to do it."

"What a wonderful way to explain meekness," Mrs. Hanford whispered to Sebbie as they sat side by side in the church service. "That describes you so well."

Sebbie couldn't answer. Her eyes were wet with tears.

ᔰ

After the service, Griffin made his way to Marco Polo, though he would have enjoyed stopping long enough to converse with Sebbie. But he would respect Mrs. Hanford's wishes and stay out of the way of Mr. Boutwell's pursuit, painful though the doing of it was. What a pompous man the young Mr. Boutwell was. The senior Mr. Boutwell didn't seem so stuffy. Did the young Mr. Boutwell take after his mother? Surely so. Known for her thorniness, Mrs.

Boutwell kept her nose in the air both figuratively and literally.

Griffin walked slowly down the steps of the white clapboard building, hoping to at least catch a glimpse of Sebbie. She looked lovely today, as always, like a spring blossom with the camellias tucked in her high collar, just like the night of the social, and on the side of her straw hat were a few more of the bright pink blossoms. Her golden curls were just so, her eyes as blue as always, and the graceful lines of her figure enhanced her simple gown.

Perhaps I could— He stopped himself, remembered the Lord's directive.

"Trust Me," the Lord had told him.

I'll do that, Lord. I definitely need Your help.

He heard Marco Polo's whinny and smiled as he thought of the steed's fine stature and form. He pressed through the crowd, greeting people, stopping for introductions here and there. Finally he was in the area reserved for the horses.

"Mr. Parks," Kit shrieked from where she stood rubbing Marco Polo's neck. She thrust out her hand for a hearty handshake.

"Mr. Parks," Bertie called. She was braiding Marco Polo's mane. She didn't let go, just beamed at him and kept braiding.

"Hello, Miss Kit, Miss Bertie," Griffin said. "This is a most welcome turn of events." He was glad to see two members of the frolicsome family of ladies from Happy Acres, would always be glad to see them.

"We couldn't resist," Kit said, pointing to Marco Polo.

"Marco Polo likes it, from what I can see."

A quarter hour quickly passed as the three exchanged bits of news and pleasantries, Kit exclaiming "hallelujah" every now and then, which amused him no end.

"Kit, Bertie." Sebbie's tone held reprimand as she appeared on the scene. "Whatever are you doing?" She paused. "Mr.

Parks. It's. . .it's nice to see you." Now her tone sounded formal. "You're not bothering Mr. Parks, are you, Girls?"

"Not in the least," Griffin said. "They have my permission to attend to Marco Polo any time there's an opportunity. I'm sure Marco Polo thinks this is old homecoming week." He chuckled. "I'm certain he's missed the girls as much as they've missed him."

"Thank you for your kindness, Mr. Parks. Come, Girls. We must be on our way. Mama is waiting."

Kit and Bertie came around by Sebbie, at the ready to go.

Sebbie made no move. It was as if she were hammered and nailed to the spot. She touched the camellias in her collar, her hands—trembling?—busying over the waxy, evergreen leaves of the blossoms. "I–I'm wondering something, Mr. Parks. . . ."

"Sebbie, we'll be walking on now," Kit said, taking Bertie's arm in hers.

"I–I'm coming too." Sebbie snatched one of the camellias from her collar, rolled the stem in her fingers, seemed distracted.

"Take your time, Sebbie," Kit said, decidedly winking at Griffin out of Sebbie's view.

Griffin swallowed hard. Kit's playful wink didn't amuse him as her antics usually did. It made his heart take to pounding, for he was certain of the meaning behind it. *We want you and Sebbie to be together, Mr. Parks*, seemed to be Kit's secret signal to him.

Kit touched Sebbie's sleeve. "As I said, Sebbie, take your time. Mama's probably talking the hind legs off a billy goat about now—"

"Kit! Mind your manners."

Kit shrugged. "I didn't mean any disrespect. You know how she loves to greet people. That's all I meant. Take your time talking with Mr. Parks, Sebbie. There's no hurry.

Mama's enjoying herself, I'm sure." Then she and Bertie bounded away.

Sebbie stood there, still rolling the camellia in her fingers, still staring down at her shoes.

"You wished to speak to me, Miss Hanford?" Hope rose in his heart, but being the levelheaded man that he was, Griffin squelched it.

"Marco Polo. H–he's. . .doing well?"

"Admirably." Griffin drew a ragged breath at her nearness. She was still staring at the toes of her shoes, the hem of her skirts, the ground, anything but him. But right then, he knew—could sense it—that she no more wanted to talk about Marco Polo than he did. She wanted to talk about them. He felt like shouting one of Kit's hallelujahs, but he restrained himself. His thoughts ran in a dozen directions. It was all going to work out, the courting of Miss Hanford and the marrying of her.

"I'm glad to hear he's completely recovered."

"Who?" Griffin said distractedly.

She laughed, and then he laughed, and she smiled that brilliant smile at him, and the sun danced on the gold of her hair.

"Marco Polo," she said with a dip of her chin and a sweep of her lashes, sweetness personified. "I'm glad he's completely recovered."

"Yes, Marco Polo." Griffin exulted in the affection that seemed to flow between them.

"I fretted so when he took sick. . . ."

You were so worried, you sold your treasured wedding silk to get help for him.

"Good afternoon, Miss Hanford, Mr. Parks," said the young Mr. Boutwell as he came that way, stopped, politely tipped his bowler hat at them, and continued on.

Sebbie's grasp on her reticule was so firm, her knuckles

were white. "Good afternoon, Mr. Boutwell," she called after him, as did Griffin for politeness's sake.

"A moment ago, Miss Hanford," Griffin said softly, "you said you were wondering something. I too am wondering something. May I ask it of you?"

She gave a furtive glance after Mr. Boutwell but didn't respond.

"I promise it's not of a delicate nature. Perhaps it's more of a josh." What it really was, he told himself, was an attempt to get her to converse with him.

She nodded, a look of trust in her eyes.

"What brand are you?" He couldn't keep from smiling.

Her creamy complexion turned beet red. "Y–you heard us?"

"I couldn't help it. You see, I too was on the promenade. Your voices carried across the night air—"

"Oh dear." She bit her lip, a worried frown crossing her face.

"Let your fears be allayed. It happened at the end of the promenade. I was accompanying Mrs. Adams, the proprietor of the boardinghouse who is old enough to be my grandmother. We were the last ones to come inside. We followed you and Mr. Boutwell out. So no one heard your conversation but Mrs. Adams and me. Your private words are safe with both of us, I assure you."

"Thank you, Mr. Parks, for your understanding. And for your kindness. Unlike some I know. . ." Her voice trailed off as she looked in the direction of Mr. Boutwell.

He nodded. "A man's prejudices tell a lot about him, Miss Hanford."

"Truer words were never spoken," she admitted.

"Yes."

"Oh, why do people turn up their noses at those bound by poverty?" She clasped her hands together, her voice animated, her expression earnest. "Rich people." She let out a sound of disdain. "Why do they think themselves better than others just because of their wealth?"

"Money has the potential to do odd things to people. Sometimes it makes them act in unseemly ways. . . ."

"I take it you've come across things like this before?"

He thought of a certain young debutante who would make the perfect match for the pitiful Mr. Boutwell. They shared the same pomposity, the same haughtiness, the same coxcombry.

"Did you hear me, Mr. Parks? I asked if you've seen things like this before?"

"Yes. Most assuredly, I'm sorry to say." He smiled. "Methinks young Mr. Boutwell is a toad."

"Mr. Parks!" But she laughed heartily, and he did too.

"However, it would be inconsiderate of us to be unforgiving toward him."

"Yes, you're right."

"Perhaps he's been influenced in the wrong way," he suggested, thinking of Mrs. Boutwell and her uppity ways.

"Oh, yes."

He was sure Sebbie caught his meaning. "We must show him Christian charity."

"Yes."

"After all, we would never want to be guilty of that which he so blatantly is."

"No. We must be inclined to mercy," Sebbie added.

"Of course."

She pulled her shawl more tightly about her shoulders as the wind whipped up. "Well, I must hurry on. As I told the girls, my mother is waiting on us." She looked intently into his eyes. "I'm glad we had this conversation, Mr. Parks."

"A pleasantry, Miss Hanford."

"I'm grateful we could talk this over and that we see eye to eye. After all, we're of the same brand."

"And what brand is that?"

"We're from the same station of life."

"I thought you were going to say something about meekness."

"Meekness?"

"What the preacher spoke on this morning, remember? Meekness? It's having strength of mind, coupled with wisdom in how to use it."

Her cheeks grew as pink as the camellias at her collar, and he wondered.

They said good-bye, and he stood watching as she walked down the path to meet her family, her skirts swishing in the wind.

He was thrilled that she had finally opened up to him, so much so that he felt like leaping in the air and kicking his heels together.

My tenderhearted Sebbie. . .

"All I have to do now," he whispered to Marco Polo, who whinnied back in response, "is ask her mother for permission to court her. And after that, well, everyone knows what courting leads to."

seventeen

The next Saturday, Sebbie still had not recovered from the unsettling feelings that had surfaced during her conversation with Griffin after church. With every footfall on the wooden planks beneath her feet, Sebbie's heart cried out, Yes, No, Yes, No, Yes.

Yes to Mr. Parks's pursuit, for it would most surely be forthcoming.

No to Mr. Parks's pursuit, for it would most surely grieve Mama.

Yes.

No.

Yes.

On she *clackety-clacked* down the walkway, her soul vexed.

The pleasant camaraderie that had sprung up between them during that conversation thrilled her. The embers of love that had glowed during their correspondence had now sparked into a brightly burning flame. Thoughts of Griffin— she had taken to referring to him that way again—consumed her heart and mind, so much that all week, Mama had taken note of how distracted she seemed.

"Sebbie, are you troubled about something?" Mama had asked a couple of times, once when they were canning some corn. "You seem so quiet, more so than usual. You're preoccupied with your contemplations."

It was difficult to find an answer for her mother without revealing her true turn of mind. She felt she needed some time to sort out her feelings before she sat down and discussed them with her mother, for she intended to do so as she always did. Finally, Sebbie said, "I'm doing some deep thinking, is all, Mama."

Her mother touched Sebbie's forearm as they stood in front of the stove, the vat of water a rolling boil. " 'And the peace of God, which passeth all understanding, shall keep your hearts and minds through Christ Jesus,' " she quoted from the Bible. "The Lord will give a peace that will be so sweet, you'll marvel at it, Sebbie."

Sebbie had smiled at that bit of wisdom from her mother. The words of Scripture had quieted her troubled spirit.

Now, though, as Sebbie traversed the planked sidewalk toward Hayes's General Store, her spirit was troubled again. What to do about Griffin? What to do? Her heart dictated one thing, but her head said another. It was like a warring within her, and it was grievous. It had kept her up late for several nights in a row. Not only was she tired in mind, she was exhausted in body.

She reached for the door, and the tinkling bell signaled her coming in.

"Morning, Miss Hanford," Mr. Hayes said as she made her way toward him.

"Hello, Mr. Hayes." She put the basket she was carrying on the counter.

"What can I do for you this fine morning?"

She drew out her wares. "These handkerchief dolls. . ." She held up a finely fashioned, hand-embroidered simple doll made from a handkerchief. "I have ten of them." She touched the basket, drew out three or four, and placed them on the counter. "I was wondering, since Christmas is nearing. . ." She gestured at the strand of holly and berries in the store window. "I was wondering if these would sell. I wanted to find out if. . .if you would be interested in buying them and reselling them to your customers."

Mr. Hayes silently studied the charming handkerchief

doll, turning it this way and that, peering through his little gold glasses.

"They aren't costly, I know," Sebbie hurriedly added. "Just simple, hand-fashioned dolls." The magnificent doll in the store window—the one she had taken to calling Ophelia and Cecilia's doll—was peering at her with pale blue eyes from her perch above a toy train. There was no way she could ever purchase that doll for the girlies; but if the handkerchief dolls sold, she could at least buy them some candies for Christmas. She had taken to making the dolls during her sleepless nights as she pondered about her feelings for Griffin. By the light of the full moon streaming into her window, she had stuffed the heads and gathered the necks. By day, between chores, she had embroidered the faces and hair and tatted the lace on their skirts. At least the sleepless nights had been productive.

She held up one of the dolls and launched in again. "Mr. Hayes, I thought maybe the cowhands coming and going through these parts might be interested in them as gifts, since they're inexpensive." She could feel her face heating up. This was so humiliating. Mama had no qualms about selling her quilts. Sebbie, on the other hand, was so shy, it was like she were trying to sell him her soul. Give her a kitchen to scrub, clothes to wash, a garden to tend, but don't make her face the public like this. She detested it, especially since she was asking Mr. Hayes to do something he obviously did not want to do. Convincing was not her forte.

Please, Ground, swallow me up.

The bell on the door jangled, but she continued staring at her handkerchief dolls on the counter. Still Mr. Hayes said nothing. She gathered up the dolls, placing them one by one back into her basket.

"Well, hello, Miss Hanford," Mr. Parks's deep bass voice boomed from behind her.

Ground, you're not cooperating. Lord? Are You there? Please translate me from this spot.

"You're just the person I need to see," Mr. Parks said. "I need to inquire something of you."

"Me?" she questioned, aghast. He was the last person she wished to see. She was afraid of her telltale heart, worried that it might reveal its true feelings. Out of sight, out of mind, was what she was trying to practice with Griffin— no, Mr. Parks. Once he left here and she never saw him again, perhaps she could get him out of her mind and heart. Oh, she prayed that would happen. She couldn't live the rest of her life pining away for a man she couldn't have. It was torturous.

"What have you here?" Mr. Parks gestured at the doll Mr. Hayes was still holding.

"Miss Hanford made these herself," Mr. Hayes said. "Miss Hanford, the reason I was hesitating is because I was trying to decide how many I'll need. Can you make fifteen more in short order?"

She nearly fainted. He wanted to buy not only the ten she had with her, but fifteen besides?

"And next week, how about ten more?"

She felt like shouting hallelujah.

"That might be too taxing, though—"

"Oh, no, Mr. Hayes. I can do it."

"These are quaint," Mr. Parks said as he looked down at the little dolls in the basket. "Up north, they'd sell for a princely sum since they're hand-fashioned."

Mr. Hayes let out a loud, good-natured guffaw. "Yes, they're very nice. I think they'll sell well. So, Miss Hanford, you can do it? Keep me supplied until Christmas?"

"Yes, Sir." Sugarplums were dancing in her head, and several lengths of fabric, and two new pairs of shoes, small ones. *Oh, if only I can buy a few things for the girlies, I'll be so happy. . . .*

"Then I'll look to see you next Saturday, Miss Hanford? With more of the dolls?"

"Oh, yes." She tried to contain the enthusiasm in her voice, but it gushed out. "It'll be my pleasure, Mr. Hayes. And thank you for your kindness."

Mr. Hayes nodded, then took the dolls out of the basket in his big beefy hands, turned around, and put them on a shelf behind him. He left space between each one and swirled out their lace-trimmed skirts as he displayed them in an eye-pleasing manner.

Sebbie picked up her basket and turned to go.

"May I help you, Mr. Parks?" Mr. Hayes asked as he whirled around.

"Yes. But I need to speak with Miss Hanford first."

"Certainly."

Sebbie floated toward the door, so high were her spirits at the success of her sales.

"Sebbie?" Mr. Parks asked.

Her spirits plummeted as she sensed his nearness behind her. *Oh, Griffin, please don't torture me. Please stay away from me. If only you knew how deeply my feelings run for you; but then, you can never know. Ever. Please take your leave and hurry it up.*

"May I have a word with you?"

She paused at the door. She needed to get away from him. She needed to put distance between them. But good breeding dictated that she employ proper manners. She turned, gave him a quick glance, and reluctantly nodded. She fiddled with the tie of her shawl.

"We could speak outside," he suggested. "Will that be agreeable to you?"

She nodded again, reaching for the door handle.

Outside, they stood side by side in the bright sunlight. She didn't say a word, couldn't, not with him this near. She didn't trust her voice.

"I need to see your mother about a matter, and I was wondering—"

"My mother?" Sebbie's mother was at home. A thousand thoughts flew through her mind, all too jumbled to decipher. What could he want with Mama? He had boarded with them, and he had seen Mama selling quilts. Maybe it had something to do with business. But it didn't matter. Sebbie could not bear to see him again today or any other day, and especially not at Happy Acres.

"I presume you're heading home shortly?"

She gave a slow nod.

"May I call on Mrs. Hanford this afternoon at three?"

She dropped the basket she was holding, and he swooped down and picked it up, then held fast to it.

She stared at the planks beneath her feet. She didn't want him to come to Happy Acres. He had no right to intrude on their property—no, her heart. He had no right to inflict himself on her. Her emotions were all atwitter, overwrought. She decided she would ward him off for good.

"No, you may not." A firmness came into her voice that surprised even her. There. She'd done it. Little ol' meek her.

"No?" His eyebrows shot up. "No, you said?"

"It. . .it wouldn't be convenient." She wasn't being untruthful. She and her mother had already laid plans to shake the rugs after the noon dinner. It was a difficult chore, and messy besides. Dirt would be flying everywhere, especially if there was any wind. And they always washed their hair afterward, even though they tied up their heads during the cleaning. And washing their hair meant there would be water to draw and transport, and then they would have to sit in the sun and dry their hair so they wouldn't catch cold with wet locks. That was the only pleasant part about the whole process, an hour or so of rest and relaxation. Ah, she welcomed the thought, especially after the short nights she'd been experiencing.

"I see." Mr. Parks's brows drew together, as if he were in deep contemplation. Then he handed her the basket he was still holding, his fingers seeming to fumble at the effort. "Very well, Miss Hanford." He tipped his hat. "Good day." He turned and walked briskly down the walk.

Sebbie trudged along the walk in the opposite direction, her heart sorrowful, more than flesh and blood could bear.

❧

Griffin walked briskly toward the boardinghouse, feeling nearly as consternated as he had the night the pretty debutante up north had tried her tricks on him. Her ploys had sickened him. He had washed his hands of her that evening, and he would now wash his hands of Sebbie Hanford.

What was going on with her? Last week, when they'd conversed after the church service, she was all sunshine and smiles. Today, she was an ice maiden. Why, her actions bordered on rudeness, what with her clipped words and her chin thrust high in the air.

That smote his heart all the more, to think of the tenderhearted Sebbie being of that vein. But apparently, her true colors were revealed today. Surely he had misjudged her this entire time. He thought her all good breeding and manners despite the family's penury. He thought her good-hearted despite the slights the family had had to bear.

But more important than those things, far more important, he had thought her affections were toward him, or at least growing that way. He assumed their hearts would be bound together for all eternity.

Well, apparently he'd thought wrong. He was so agitated, he felt like a wild stallion roaming the pasture. Yes, he would wash his hands of Sebbie Hanford. After today, he hoped never to set eyes on her again.

Evidently, she was shallow—fickle, even—for certainly her actions proved this. Into his mind popped an image of Mrs.

Adams's house cat. Yesterday, as Griffin entered the boarding-house, he had been amused at Tom Cat's buffoonery. Poor Tom Cat had been racing through the lobby, skittering across the polished wooden floors, sliding when he lost his footing, as he pursued a mouse. Several of the boardinghouse guests had laughed at his antics.

That's what Griffin felt like right now, Tom Cat, skittering across the floors, sliding and not being able to stop as he gave chase to the cunning mouse.

Well, he could stop this chase. Right now. And he would. He was tired of this cat-and-mouse game Sebbie was play-ing. His ire was up. Didn't Sebbie know she couldn't toy with a person's affections? That it was unseemly? Unacceptable?

"Mr. Parks!"

Griffin was startled when he heard his name called. Sebbie? Swift footfalls indicated someone was running toward him. Hope rose in his chest, but he chastised himself. He was accusing Sebbie of being fickle, and here he was being the same way. He had already made up his mind, and he would not waiver, no matter what.

"Mr. Parks!"

But his curiosity was piqued, and he whirled around.

"Mr. Parks," Bertie huffed out for the third time as she ran pell-mell toward him.

Bertie. He forced a smile. He was in no mood to see any of the Hanford ladies, but he would at least be civil to the young girl he had become endeared to.

Bertie bustled up to him in her brash way and stopped in front of him, still huffing from her strenuous run. "I saw you and Sebbie talking—"

He shrugged, unmoved, unconcerned.

"From the looks of your parting, I can only imagine what was said."

He crossed his arms over his chest and stared off into the

distance. Couldn't Bertie see that he wasn't interested in what she had to say? Right now, she was probably making small talk; but most likely, she wanted to tell him something about Marco Polo. Well, when he decided to wash his hands of Sebbie Hanford moments ago, he had also decided to wash his hands of all of them. That was the only way to handle this properly.

"Mr. Parks, I need to say something to you. May I have a moment of your time?"

"I'm in somewhat of a hurry, Bertie."

"It's something private, but something that needs to be said."

He stared hard at her. What was on the girl's mind?

"It's about Sebbie."

He swallowed deeply. "She's of no concern to me." That was a true statement. Henceforth, he would have no dealings with her, would have no cause to.

"I'm certain you'll think differently when you hear me out. Please?"

He softened when he saw the imploring look on her face. It wouldn't hurt to hear her out, he supposed. He would show the milk of human kindness, even if her sister wasn't capable of doing so—at least to him.

"Sebbie loves you with all her heart," Bertie blurted out.

He felt hot all over. He felt confused. He felt. . .he was so flustered he didn't know how he felt.

"It's true. Every word."

He continued staring, feeling ungentlemanly to do so, but he couldn't help it.

Bertie talked on, telling him she knew with a certainty that Sebbie loved him, had seen and observed things, could sense it just because. She told him that the reason Sebbie couldn't give her affections to him was because. . .because. . .

She hesitated and then explained her mother's wish that

Sebbie marry a wealthy man. She carefully pointed out that her mother was only asking this of Sebbie to rescue the family. Bertie implored him not to think harshly of Mama, that she was only watching out for the ones she loved so dearly, like a mother hen fending for her brood, that Mama had been forced into this thinking because. . .because. . .

Bertie choked out some things about their poverty that wrung his heart. She went on and on, telling him she knew Sebbie was in anguish of soul because she was trying to be an obedient daughter, yet true love was calling out to her. Sebbie's spirit was tempest-tossed, she told him; and wasn't there some way he could right things, though Bertie couldn't imagine how?

Bertie was blubbering, and he offered her his handkerchief when she fumbled in her sleeve and turned up nothing. She dabbed at her tears and repeated that Sebbie loved him.

"Now, now, Bertie, don't cry. Everything will work out."

"It will, Mr. Parks?"

"Call me Griffin."

"Griffin?" She looked up at him, wonderment in her gaze. Then she smiled broadly, her eyes glistening with tears. "Oh, yes, Griffin."

"You go along now." He patted her forearm. "Go find Sebbie, and be on your way home. I've some thinking to do."

Bertie turned then and walked away, her steps slow.

"Bertie?"

She pivoted and faced him.

"Keep our conversation in confidence, you hear?"

"Yes, Sir."

"Don't tell anyone about it, you understand?"

"No, Sir. I won't."

"All will be well."

"Yes. . .Griffin. All will be well." She smiled once more, then turned and fairly skittered away.

On down the wooden sidewalk, Griffin leaped in the air.
And he kicked his heels together.

And he even let out a cowhand "Yippee yi, yippee yay,
yippee yo," not caring if anyone saw or heard.

eighteen

That afternoon, armed with the comforting knowledge Bertie had conveyed, Griffin made his way to the Hanfords, a happiness seeping over his being and settling into his bones. What a fitting name for the Hanfords' home: Happy Acres.

Today, this very hour, he would ask Mrs. Hanford for permission to court Sebbie and also for permission to ask for her hand in marriage when the time came. He felt like clicking his heels again, only he couldn't. Marco Polo might not take too kindly to that.

He envisioned his and Sebbie's wedding, then the weeks and months that would follow and the happiness that would be theirs, then their future together as the years stretched out ahead of them. He would build a magnificent house for the Hanfords, and they would all live in it in grand style. As time progressed, the girls and girlies would grow to maturation and in turn be courted by proper young gentlemen.

He squelched a smile, thinking of headstrong Kit and boisterous Bertie and shy Cecilia and Ophelia—well, Cecilia was shy, anyway.

How would love come to each of them? To Kit? Bertie? Cecilia? Ophelia? It was a pleasant thought to ponder as he envisioned young men coming to call at the grand house he intended to build, with its wide front porch and oak door with the oval window in it and the regal staircase that would have a curve, not a landing. Perhaps the girls and girlies might even choose to have their weddings in the house, and he saw them in his mind's eye coming down the steps dressed in a cloud of white with Sebbie playing the bridal march in the background.

When the young men came to call, they would listen to different ones of the girls playing the piano, and then they would enjoy the party dainties offered them as they came to know the Hanford girls. Sebbie would host soirees and parties often, and she and her mother and the girls would entertain their friends, and the house would be abuzz with social activities always.

And down through the years, God would bless him and Sebbie with girls of their own—and boys too. God would give them however many children He saw fit, and those children would add to the liveliness of the household.

It would be almost heaven.

Almost Heaven?

That's what he would call his ranch. If Happy Acres was a good name for the Hanfords' house, Almost Heaven was superb for his.

Almost Heaven. He liked the ring it had to it. But more than that, he liked the meaning behind it.

As he cantered along on Marco Polo, he thought about Bertie's revelation that morning. "Isn't there some way you can work things out?" Bertie had asked.

The surest way to work things out was to reveal his standing to them, and all would be sugarplums and icing on the cake. If Sebbie knew with a surety that he could save her family from privation, she would gladly receive his affections. And if Mrs. Hanford knew, he was sure she would grant her hearty approval.

Mrs. Hanford, I have the wherewithal to set your family up in grand style, so will you allow me to pursue your daughter? Sebbie, I have riches such as you cannot imagine, so will you marry me?

But he couldn't do that. It was too indelicate. He could envision the scene now, crass to his way of thinking, gruesome even. Knowing these things about him—before the proposal was put to them—would threaten their tender sensitivities. It would put to question their moral principles, lay a trap for their ethics. He would be forcing them to sit on a barrel of gunpowder. Then, if they chose to do as he asked because of his wealth and provision, or even if they chose to do as he asked because of his love, there would always be a yoke around his and Sebbie's necks. Their marriage would be on a sandy foundation, unstable from the start.

No, he could not do that to them. He refused to put them in such a precarious spot.

But how exactly would he handle it, the question he wished to put to Sebbie's mother? "Can I convince Mrs. Hanford to let me court Sebbie? Will she allow me to do this?"

Seeing their house looming ahead, he knew he would have his answer soon.

As he rode up to the hitching post in front of the Hanfords' house, Griffin thought back to the day he had come to Happy Acres to retrieve Marco Polo after Sebbie boarded him, when he saw no signs of visible activity, and he had wondered. Today was the same way. All was quiet: not a squeal to be heard from the twins, not a shout from Bertie, not a hallelujah from Kit.

He didn't expect to hear anything from Sebbie. She was quiet much of the time. That only made him love her more, his tender-hearted girl.

He decided to do as he had done before. He tied Marco Polo to the post in front and walked toward the back. As he rounded the corner of the house, the sight he encountered made him catch his breath and lean heavily against the weathered boards.

Sebbie. In her glory!

She was sitting on a blanket, her golden curls spread across her shoulders and down her back, glistening so brightly in the sun he felt the urge to cup his hands over his eyes. His heart beat fast in his chest.

His first thought—when at last he could think—was to flee, to run back to Marco Polo and get away as quickly as possible. It simply wasn't fitting for a man to see a woman like that.

In her glory.

But he couldn't move a muscle. He might as well be lassoed and tied up. All he could think of was his Sebbie-girl as he stared at her, and how that soon he would take her in his arms and proclaim his love for her. Then he would provide her with every pleasurable thing he could think of—for the rest of her life. And her family too.

He turned to retrace his steps, slow-like, quiet as a burglar, so Sebbie would never know he saw her like that. He wouldn't flee back to town, but he would knock on the front door, proper-like, and give her warning. He would never embarrass her.

"Mr. Parks!" Sebbie shrieked.

He turned around, saw that she was hurriedly gathering up her things. A hairbrush? A towel? Then she was flying across the raked path toward the back door, her golden locks bouncing against her in her hurry. In a flick of the eye, she was inside the house.

You lout, he told himself. *Now, you've gone and done it.*

There was nothing to do but follow the plan he had decided on. He made his way to the front porch, walked nearly tiptoe up the steps, feeling at a disadvantage from the start of his mission. He knocked firmly on the door and heard commotion inside followed by whispered voices.

After long minutes, the door sprang open in front of him.

"Mr. Parks?" Mrs. Hanford asked, her tone sounding formal.

"Mrs. Hanford." He banged his hat against his leg over and over, at a loss for words. He stopped the banging when

he realized what he was doing. "Good afternoon." He wondered about Mrs. Hanford's appearance. Her hair was most
assuredly wet. But it was in its usual topknot though some
tendrils were spilling down around her face.

"Good. . .good afternoon to you." She paused, then thrust
the door open wide. "Won't you. . .won't you come in?"

"I suppose Sebbie. . .Miss Hanford. . .is inside?"

"Yes." Mrs. Hanford's cheeks grew pink.

"I've come to speak with you. Out of Miss Hanford's hearing."

"I see."

"I've a matter of import to discuss."

She looked around furtively, first inside, then outside.
"The chairs in the yard—"

"That's a fine spot, Mrs. Hanford." He didn't mean to cut
her off, but that was the perfect place for their discussion. He
knew Sebbie would not be able to hear them from the house.

"I'll be there directly, then."

"Thank you. Take your time." Griffin made his way down
the steps and out to the two chairs sitting under the long
limb of the towering oak tree, feeling warm with love, but
also cold with trepidation. He must convince Mrs. Hanford
of what he wanted to do without revealing his financial situation. But it was such a formidable task.

Directly, Mrs. Hanford came down the steps, and he
jumped to his feet and dipped his chin, smiling gently at her.
Her topknot was perfect this time, the sides of her hair rigidly
held back by combs. Her apron had been removed, and in her
hands she carried a tray with two glasses filled with water.

She silently offered him a glass, and he took it. She said
not a word to him, only a half-smile on her lips. They both
took their seats, and Mrs. Hanford put the tray on the
ground, the second glass—hers—untouched. For a moment,
silence reigned save for the birdsong high above them.

"Mrs. Hanford, I trust you and your family had a good

day." He felt silly. They had already greeted each other with those words.

"Yes, we have," she said with politeness. She could be relied on to display proper etiquette always. "And you, Mr. Parks?"

"A most enjoyable one." Today would stand out in his memory for all time. It marked the day he was sure of Sebbie's love for him. "It's a pleasant day." He looked up into the oak tree whose leaves were still green and unshed. Falling leaves usually occurred toward spring here in Florida, he knew. "Not too chilly and not too hot. Just right, to my way of thinking."

Mrs. Hanford, ever the talkative one, only studied her demurely folded hands. After long moments, she brightened. "When Sebbie and Bertie got back from town, Bertie went with Kit and the girlies to pick some late blackberries. I'm hoping to make a little jam, if they find enough. While they've been gone, Sebbie and I beat all the rugs. It's a messy chore that's best if only two are involved." She touched the sides of her hair. "Afterward, it means. . .well, it means more chores."

He knew exactly what she was referring to. Washing the rugs was a filthy job he had seen his mother's maids perform. Evidently for Sebbie and her mother, it meant washing their hair afterward. It also meant drying it in the sun, and the vision of Sebbie with her glorious golden curls about her shoulders invaded his heart again. He could only imagine what her luscious locks would feel like. He drew in a ragged breath.

"But you didn't come here to talk about the girls and the girlies and the chores around this place." Mrs. Hanford smoothed her skirts and squared her shoulders, rounded though they were. She looked directly at him. "Just what did you come here for, Mr. Parks?"

The drill sergeant was before him. And understandably so. A glance in the direction of their humble home, a quick sweep of the decaying bunkhouse to the side, a long look at the barn whose roof needed attention—all made the sense of how dire things were at Happy Acres wash over him with fresh poignancy.

"Mrs. Hanford, I'll not beat around the bush." He too squared his shoulders. "I've come to talk about your daughter. I love her more than words can say." He complimented Sebbie, pointing out her good qualities, which were the very things he sought in a wife. He said he loved Sebbie with his whole being and that she meant the world to him. "I wish to ask your permission to court her and then to ask for her hand in marriage when the time is right."

"I knew you came here for that."

"You did?" He was surprised. All he had ever asked her about Sebbie was for permission to escort her to the town social. How could she know his intentions now?

"A mother knows these things."

He nodded.

"Then you understand?"

She didn't respond. She reached down and picked up her water glass, took a long, slow swallow, took another one, placed it back on the tray on the ground.

Griffin resisted tapping his toe on the hard-packed dirt under his chair. What was Mrs. Hanford thinking about? Then he knew, deep in his soul. She was remembering their hardships, contemplating their pauperism, fretting over their future. Was she envisioning a life of poverty for her firstborn whom she loved so much? A life such as she herself had endured? For Griffin would be the one forcing this life upon Sebbie, according to Mrs. Hanford's way of thinking. He was putting her between a hawk and a buzzard by asking what he did.

Like Christian in *Pilgrim's Progress*, he plummeted to the depths of the slough of despond. Oh, if only he could tell all. If only he could allay her fears and worries, put an end to her pain. But he couldn't.

"Though Sebbie is twenty," Mrs. Hanford observed, "that doesn't mean she's unclaimed because of a flaw—"

"No, of course not."

"It's because there are so few unattached young men in these parts."

"Yes, most assuredly."

"If we lived someplace else, where eligible young men abounded, why, she would have her pick—"

"Gentlemen callers would surround her like bees near honey."

Mrs. Hanford nodded vigorously. "I had hoped. . ." Her voice trailed off as she stared out at the pasture surrounding the house. "For the first time in my life, I'm at a loss for words."

Griffin leaned forward. He repeated how much he loved Sebbie. He named her qualities again, extolling her beauty of face but far more than that, her beauty of spirit. He pledged that he would provide as well as possible for Sebbie, would even help the family to the best of his abilities. He expressed his deep affection for the girls and girlies, even for Mrs. Hanford herself.

Still, she said nothing, but kept staring at the pastureland.

"It's a matter of trust, isn't it?" he asked.

"It's more than that, far more. You're young. You've not seen what I've seen. You've not experienced what age teaches you. You've not known what I've known." Her expression changed from quiet nonchalance to one of passion and fire. "Oh, but you will, Mr. Parks. Mark my words. You will. For if you live on a ranch any length of time, you'll soon come to know of the harshness of life, the things unforeseen and unplanned that befall you. Yes, mark my words, Mr. Parks, a reckoning is in the future for you."

He sank back against the slats of the chair, listening without flinching, but inside he was writhing. Her words were true, given her circumstances. She could see no farther than her own experiences and the life she had lived out. If only. . .

But he chided himself again. He must find a way to reach her, to convince her.

She stood up, took a pensive pose, tapped on her bottom lip. "I'll tell you what I'm going to do."

He stood up too. "Which is?"

"Your love for Sebbie is true—"

"A mother knows these things, right?" He smiled, feeling a bit playful and certainly hopeful, remembering when she had said that earlier.

She was somber as a skeleton. "As I said, I'm convinced that your love for Sebbie is true. And strong. I was young once. I remember. I can see what's so plainly before me. However, I'm going to put the choice on Sebbie's shoulders. After all, it is her life. She must be the one to decide."

He didn't know what to think, how to feel. He knew the deep devotion between mother and daughter. He knew the strong bonds that tied them together. He knew the way Sebbie had been raised, to obey her parents no matter what she wanted to do—just as nearly every family of good stock raised their children. It was an accepted fact, a principle a person followed without question, doing what parents directed.

He drew in another deep breath, something he had done quite a bit of today. What would Sebbie do? What would she decide? The thought made him quiver.

"You may talk with her yourself. Tomorrow afternoon at this same time."

Now, he was the one who wasn't responding.

"I'll try to give you and Sebbie some privacy in which to discuss these things. I'll plan a jaunt for the girls and girlies." Mrs. Hanford looked down. With the toe of her shoe, she moved an acorn a couple of inches to the right. She looked up. "Mr. Parks?"

"Thank you for your. . .your understanding. And. . .and for your kindness to me, Mrs. Hanford. Whatever transpires between Sebbie and me, I'll always be appreciative of that. And I'll always have fond memories of my stay at Happy Acres."

"Very well then, Mr. Parks."

A quarter hour later, he was riding back to town.

"I'll always have fond memories of my stay at Happy Acres," he had told Mrs. Hanford.

He rethought that. "If Sebbie refuses me, the memories of my stay at Happy Acres will be the most painful I will ever have to endure."

❧

That night, Sebbie drew a weary sigh as she took off her dress and shift and put on her nightgown. She and her mother had beaten the rugs till their arms ached, dirt flying everywhere. Though she didn't mind hard work—it was a part of life that she understood and accepted—she detested this chore. She was glad it was over and done with.

As she plaited her freshly washed hair in two long braids, she looked across the room and saw that Kit and Bertie were already asleep in the wide bed they shared. The two of them were such flurries of activity all day, it was no wonder they went out like a lamp as soon as their heads hit the pillow at night.

"Sebbie?" came her mother's whisper at the door, which stood ajar.

Sebbie walked to the door. "Mama? You need me?" Her mother stood in the wide, dim hallway, looking serious, her smile absent. But there were love and kindness in her eyes.

"Are you too tired to talk a few minutes?"

"No, of course not." Sebbie reached for her wrapper where it hung on a nail behind the door and hurriedly thrust her arms into it and tied the sash. What did her mother want to say to her? This late? What was this all about? Did it have something to do with Griffin? Her face grew warm thinking of him happening upon her that afternoon with her hair down. She knew for a certainty if she peered into a mirror right now, her face would be beet red. This afternoon, Griffin had come here for a purpose. No one made the trip to Happy Acres without a reason. But she didn't know what that reason was. Was she about to find out? Mama hadn't breathed a word.

"Let's go to the kitchen," Mama whispered.

When both of them reached the kitchen—Sebbie carrying a lamp to light the way—they sat down facing each other across the table, the lamp in the middle.

"I'm wondering what it is you need to tell me, Mama." Sebbie settled back against her chair.

"I'm sorry to keep you up—"

"I wasn't anticipating going right to sleep."

"Oh?"

"Some nights it takes me forever to enter dreamland."

Her mother nodded.

Sebbie adjusted the wick in the lamp; and the flame grew, then returned to its normal size.

"I planned to talk with you after supper but—"

"The twins prevented it." Sebbie laughed as she recalled the funny picture the little tykes had made at dusk when they traipsed up the porch steps covered in mud. Seems they had decided to set up a mud bakery after supper, and then they decided to see what mud looked like smeared on their arms and legs. It was even on their faces. Sebbie laughed harder when she thought about the dark Florida loam deeply embedded in their ears.

"I thought we never would get all of that mud scrubbed off of them. And out of them." Mama chuckled. "But we finally did."

Sebbie rolled her eyes. "Four buckets of water. Who would ever think it would take that much to bathe two little girls?"

"And then it was time to rustle them up a snack and read them a bedtime story. And then you helped me get the bulk of Sunday dinner prepared for tomorrow—"

"So we can eat as soon as we get home from church."

"Isn't it wonderful we're having the parson come through again? This near to the last time he came?"

Sebbie nodded. "And after church tomorrow, all we have to do is heat up the greens and fried chicken and then butter the corn bread and toast it a little, and then open some applesauce. We can do it in a jiffy. That'll please the girls and girlies—"

"Since they're always so hungry—around the clock, it seems." Mama's expression changed back to the serious look she had worn earlier. "And now it's nearly ten o'clock." She leaned forward and folded her arms on the table. "Sebbie, I need to talk to you about something very serious."

"I assumed as much."

"It concerns Mr. Parks."

"Yes, I thought so."

Her mother gave her that knowing nod.

"It only stands to reason that he came here this afternoon to talk to you about something of import," Sebbie said. "I doubt it was about Marco Polo."

"No."

"So, what was it?"

"He loves you dearly. . . ."

Sebbie's heart pounded.

"He wants permission to court you. . . ."

Sebbie's breath came in short little gasps.

"And when the time comes, to ask for your hand in marriage."

Sebbie's eyes misted. "And. . .and what did you tell him, Mama?"

"Remember when I told you my Christmas wish, when

little Cecilia was talking about her Christmas wish—about wishing for the doll in the store window?"

"Yes." How could she forget?

"Remember when I said I wished that you would marry a well-to-do man and help our family?"

"Yes." How could she not remember that—such a fearsome thing her mother had asked of her? She drummed her fingers on the table. *What did Mama tell Griffin when he came asking for her permission to. . .to court and propose? What did Mama say to him? Apparently, it wasn't good news. Otherwise, Griffin would have spoken with me before he left, wouldn't he?*

"You know the reasons for my wish—"

"Yes." Sebbie knew every last one of them, and she hoped her mother wouldn't go over the reasons now, about the hardships she had endured following Jed "Wanderlust" Hanford to the wilds of Florida, about the losing of him that was the worst hardship of all, about the years since when Mama had worked her fingers to the bone trying to keep body and soul together for six people.

But her mother did recount the reasons, every last one of them. Finally, she said, "Mr. Parks—"

"What did you tell him, Mama?" Sebbie was sorry for interrupting. She should have given her mother a chance to voice her opinion. Although Sebbie tried to keep the eagerness out of her voice, she couldn't help it. "What's the verdict?" she asked hurriedly, unable to wait a moment more.

"I said. . .I said. . ."

Sebbie hung on her mother's every word. "What? What did you tell him?"

"I said you'll have to be the one to make the decision."

Sebbie felt like a thousand-pound weight had just hit her. "But Mama, knowing what you wish—"

"It's your life, Sebbie. You must decide. I—I won't. . .interfere." Mama folded her hands into a tight clasp.

"Oh, Mama, what must I do?"

Trembling, Mama folded her arms across her chest.

Sebbie fiddled with the edge of the cloth covering the table. She noticed a few stitches had come undone at the hem. She must remember to sew them. A stitch in time saves nine, her mother always said. She jolted out of her reverie. Here she was at the most momentous occasion of her life, and yet she was thinking about sewing and stitches and saving one from added work.

"As I said, Sebbie, you must weigh everything and then decide."

Sebbie fiddled with the tablecloth again. "I–I love him too, Mama. With all my heart." She glanced up at her mother, then down again at the hem she was holding in her hand. "I tried not to, honest I did. But it was too strong, the love I felt for him." She stood up, and the chair nearly fell over backward with her quick movement. She righted it and grasped the back. "Mama, I love Griffin Parks with the same kind of love you loved Papa."

Her mother started to say something, but Sebbie cut her off.

"I saw a deep, abiding love between you and Papa, a love that said, 'I'll go through the thick and thin of life with you. I'll never leave you nor forsake you. "Whither thou goest, I will go." You are my first, my last, my only true love.' "

"Beautifully put," her mother said quietly.

"That's the kind of love you had for Papa, isn't it? And the kind of love he had for you?"

"Yes."

"That's the kind of love I have for Griffin."

Her mother gave her that knowing nod for the third time that night.

"But I can't marry him."

Her mother looked at her sharply.

"Unless I have your blessing." Sebbie sank to her chair and pulled it toward her mother with a clatter, not caring if the noise woke the family or not. She gathered her mother's hands in her own, kneading them like dough. "I'll not be a disobedient daughter, Mama. You've raised me too well. I won't do that to you."

Her mother's gaze was fixed on the window that seemed to be a black hole in the dark of night.

"Mama? Do you hear me? I must have your blessing if Griffin and I are to become man and wife."

Now her mother was kneading Sebbie's hands, over and over.

"Otherwise, I'll turn him down, and we will never see each other again."

On and on Mama kneaded Sebbie's hands, first her fingers, then her palms, then her wrists, then her fingers again. "I remember the first time I met your father. . .Jed. Oh, Sebbie, our love was a brightly burning bonfire almost from the very beginning. It was thrilling. . . ."

I know the feeling.

"He was so handsome. Tall with a regal bearing. And he had such strength of character."

I know another man just like him.

"Sebbie?" Her mother hugged her. Hard. Then she wiped her eyes that were fast filling with tears. "True love is rewarding, no matter what you face."

Sebbie nodded in her mother's tight embrace, the pleasant scent of Mama's freshly washed hair filling her nostrils.

"I grant my approval for you and Griffin to marry."

Sebbie thought her heart would burst in two from happiness.

"And I bestow a blessing on your union. . .a bountiful one."

"Oh, thank you, Mama."

Still embracing, Mama patted Sebbie's hair, played with the long braids on each side. "I don't know what's ahead for you. Or for all of us, for that matter. But I do know one thing, my dear."

"What's that?"

"Your love will be heavenly."

nineteen

Sebbie was watching from her bedroom window as Griffin rode into the yard the next afternoon, and her heart beat nearly out of her chest. The new knowledge she was privy to thrilled her.

"Griffin loves me." She did a little two-step on the hard wooden floor, her heels coming together with a *thwack-thwack-thwack*.

"Hallelujah," she sang out. She smiled as she fiddled with the camellias stuck in her collar. She plucked another one from the bouquet on the bureau and put it in her hair. "Griffin loves me. And I love him."

A quarter hour later, she was outside with everyone in the cool afternoon air. It had turned chilly overnight, and it felt just right for the Christmas season upon them. They were all there—Mama, Kit, Bertie, the twins. . .and Griffin.

She greeted him, carefully avoiding his eyes, shy with her newfound knowledge. How she would acknowledge—how they would both acknowledge—their love for each other, she had no idea. But the delightful prospect put a glow in her heart and anticipation in her spirit that sent tingles racing up her spine.

The twins were jumping up and down, begging Griffin to swing them in the air; and Kit and Bertie were shouting over the twins' clamor, asking him about Marco Polo. Mama was trying to give instructions to Kit and Bertie, who were to take the girlies on an outing, only they weren't listening. Sebbie stood quietly to the side, observing the whole happy throng.

Before Sebbie knew what was happening, Griffin had arranged for him and Sebbie to go on the outing too. They were going to hunt for a Christmas tree, what with the holiday fast approaching.

"Why, Mr. Parks?" Mama asked him quietly, but Sebbie overheard in the noisy din. "I thought you wanted to talk with Sebbie? Alone."

"I do," he replied, a twinkle in his eye. "And I will."

So all of them set off save for Mama, who pleaded a much-needed nap. The party of six stuffed into the Hanfords' rickety wagon, their closeness welcoming in the crisp December air.

"It's freezing," Bertie said from behind Griffin, who sat on the buckboard, driving. "The weather changed during the night. Yesterday, we were in shirt sleeves, as Papa used to say."

Kit stuck her head between Sebbie and Griffin. "And today, we're in long underwear—"

"Kit!" Sebbie exclaimed, but they all laughed. Shivering, she fastened the top button of her coat, her heart pounding at Griffin's nearness. *Soon, I'll be telling you of my love, Griffin.* She shivered again, and it wasn't because of the cold.

"Yes, it's mighty chilly today." Griffin gave out an exaggerated *b-r-r-r-r.* "The mercury must be down to fifty-five." He chuckled. "Up north, they're having snowstorms right now. I believe we can all endure this freezing weather." He threw Bertie a lighthearted wink. "Ah, Florida."

All afternoon, they traipsed through the woods, hunting for the perfect pine tree, then cutting it down, laughing and singing all the while. Sebbie said very little and sang very little, letting her heart do all the talking and singing. Somehow, she sensed Griffin knew this.

Griffin put the small pine tree on the back of the wagon, and then Sebbie pulled out a basket from inside the wagon box. She didn't touch the package in the brown wrapper that Griffin had brought.

"Time for some refreshment," she said, and all gathered around. She gave instructions for Kit and Bertie to spread a blanket and for the girlies to be seated, and then she gave out the sugar cookies she had made the day before—their first Christmas treat of the season. Her handkerchief dolls had sold well, well enough that she had been able to buy some sugar, as well as some candies and small trinkets for the girlies and Kit and Bertie. Those would go in their Christmas stockings for Christmas morning.

As she doled out the cookies, she felt proud. She had taken great pains with them, cutting them out in palm-tree shapes and alligators, like the ones her mother had made when she was a little girl. A cup of water each, and their refreshments were complete.

The girlies exclaimed at the simple treat, as did Kit and Bertie.

Sebbie sat down and ate a cookie, the familiar warmth for her family seeping over her. *It takes so little to satisfy them. How I wish I could give them more.*

From the brown paper wrapper, Griffin produced a jar of apple cider and then took a seat on the blanket, and they exclaimed all the more. When he pulled out a pan with miniature iced cakes on them, they all oohed and ahhed.

"They're too fancy to eat," little Cecilia said, wonderment in her eyes as she peered at the pan.

"Not for me." Kit reached for one and bit into it with lightning speed.

"Kit!" Sebbie exclaimed. "Mind your manners," she whispered.

"Let her have her fill," Griffin said, a softness to his expression. "There are plenty of them. And plenty more where they came from."

"Where did they come from?" Bertie asked, gobbling her first one almost as fast as Kit was finishing her second.

"Mrs. Adams made them for me."

Little tingles danced up Sebbie's spine as their gazes locked across the blanket. *Oh, Griffin, how kind, how thoughtful. . .how wonderful you are.*

Soon, they were in the rickety wagon headed back toward Happy Acres, happiness filling every voice.

Three-quarters of an hour later, just as dusk was settling, they reached home and unloaded the Christmas tree, the girls and girlies making for the house with unbounded haste, laughing and shouting about the paper chains they were planning to make for the tree. The perfume of perking coffee wafted through the air, and Sebbie knew Mama was in the kitchen warming dinner leavings—corn bread and collard greens, though the fried chicken was long gone.

Griffin touched Sebbie's forearm as she reached for the picnic basket. More tingles danced up her spine.

"May I have a word with you?" he said quietly from where he stood beside the wagon, and she thought her heart would burst out of its resting place as their eyes met.

Time stood still.

Words unspoken passed between them.

"I thought we would have a chance to talk this afternoon." His deep bass voice was a mere whisper. "But time got away."

She nodded.

Facing her, he took her hands in his, and she felt sure she was going to swoon. "Sebbie, your mother and I had a long discussion yesterday afternoon—"

"I know," she blurted out, so unlike her, but she couldn't keep down her enthusiasm. "She told me all about it."

"Is that right?"

"Yes. She said. . .she said. . ." She felt her cheeks grow warm, even though a brisk breeze swirled about them, and she looked down at her shoes. "She said it's up to me."

"She did?"

"Yes. She reminded me of something she once told me, sort of a wish she has. I won't go into it, but it has to do with my. . .my matrimonial inclinations." All of a sudden, she was a chatterbox. "Her wish. . .her desire for me has direct bearing on our family. She went on and on about her reasons for her wish—"

"And how do you feel about it?"

"I feel. . .I feel. . ."

He lifted her chin to meet his gaze. "Sebbie, I love you— deeply."

"I–I told Mama. . .I love you too, with everything that's within me." She brushed at the mist in her eyes and continued, so impassioned did she feel. "I told her I tried not to love you. I really did, but it was too strong, this. . .this feeling that started growing in my heart the first day you came here. I told her I loved you as much as she loved Papa. I said I had that same deep, abiding love she had for him, the kind of love that says, 'I'll go through the thick and thin of life with you. I'll never leave you nor forsake you. "Whither thou goest, I will go." You are my first, my last, my only true love—' "

His lips brushing hers cut off her words.

"Oh, Griffin," she finally said, her heart singing so loudly she was sure he could hear it.

He didn't say anything for a long moment, and neither did she. They just stood there, in each other's tender embrace.

"And then what did you say?" He drew back from her and smiled, caressing her cheek with the back of his hand.

"I told her I needed her blessing. I told her I wouldn't be a disobedient daughter and go against her wishes—"

"And what did she say?"

She stared into his eyes and smiled as wide a smile as ever a face could smile. "She told me. . .she said. . .she said that our love will be heavenly."

twenty

Only a few more days, and it would be Christmas, Sebbie thought with a smile as she stood in front of the bureau and gave the finishing touches to her chignon. This afternoon, a Friday, they were all going to the white clapboard building to see the children recite. All had been invited, even the townspeople, and it was expected to be as large a crowd as at the social after Thanksgiving. There would be fun and games and plenty of party dainties to eat.

There would also be Griffin.

The thought thrilled her. She hadn't seen him since last Sunday afternoon, when she had gushed out her feelings for him as she stood by the wagon and he revealed his love to her. She would see him today in not more than an hour. Every moment away from him pained her. She longed to be with him morning, noon, and night.

She waltzed across the room, her hands in the air as if on his shoulders, and she swished this way and that, singing a romance, a lover's tune she had heard her mother sing long ago:

> "*Love is in the air*
> *And I don't have a care,*
> *My heart has found true love,*
> *With the one sent from above.*'"

"'Love is in the air,'" she sang again. "'And I don't have a care.'" She sang that line slowly, its meaning hitting her with stark reality, and she stopped her little waltz in midstride and dropped her arms. *But I do have a care. My family.*

She dawdled back to the bureau, nearly dragging her feet, feeling almost dazed. *What is my love for Griffin costing me? Costing the girls? The girlies?*

The door burst open, and Ophelia and Cecilia came running in. "Hurry, Sebbie," Ophelia piped up.

"You-uh the only one who isn't weddy," Cecilia lisped.

"I heard you singing," Ophelia said. "Sing your song again, Sebbie, please?" She tugged on Sebbie's skirts.

"Careful, Girlie. You'll muss me." She smoothed the gathers at the waist of her mother's made-over blue silk, the same one she had worn to the Thanksgiving social, ran her hands down her sides, and fluffed her sleeves at the elbows.

"Please, Sebbie," Cecilia said. "Sing it fo-uh us again."

One look in those trusting cornflower blue eyes, and Sebbie started singing:

> " *Love is in the air*
> *And I don't have a care,*
> *My heart has found true love,*
> *With the one sent from above.*' "

" 'My heart has found true love—' " Ophelia belted out the lyrics as she thrust her arm to her side with a touch of drama.

" 'With the one sent from above,' " Cecilia finished. "I like that song, Sebbie," she proclaimed.

"With the one sent from above," Sebbie softly sang. She picked up her coat, put her reticule on her arm, gathered the girlies, and guided them out the door.

All the way to the party as they bumped along in the wagon, she kept her mind on the fourth line of the stanza, not the second. "*With the one sent from above.*"

In her heart she sang it over and over with gusto, passion, feeling that truly it was so.

After the recitations and games, Sebbie took the plate of party dainties Griffin brought her, and they found seats together against the south wall of the building. They conversed quietly, barely taking their eyes off each other as they partook of the refreshments.

She was so engrossed in him, she hardly knew what she was eating. She was proud of her boldness tonight. That's what she called it. Instead of being the shy soul she always was with Griffin, this time she looked at him with unconcealed affection, and it was as if she were drinking in the sight of him, like the old song said. She relished every moment in his presence.

So this is what love is. So this is how love feels.

She could go forty forevers feeling like this, enjoying his luscious nearness, and his dear countenance, and his sweet—

"Well, well," clucked Mrs. Boutwell, seeming to appear from out of nowhere. She rocked on her shoes in front of them, heel to toe and toe to heel, over and over again.

Griffin stood to his feet, nearly toppling the plate in his hand. He gave her a nod of politeness. "Good afternoon, Mrs. Boutwell."

"Hello, Mrs. Boutwell," Sebbie spoke up. "A pleasure to see you today."

"Enjoying the party? Take your seat, Mr. Parks. There's no need to trouble yourself."

"Won't you have a seat?" He gestured at the empty chair beside him as he sat back down.

"Dear me, no. I haven't been to the refreshment table yet. I see that you have." She towered over them, peering down at their plates, her hawklike nose high in the air.

Griffin put his plate on the empty chair, his fork clattering against it, and made a move to rise again. "May I get you a plate, Mrs. Boutwell? I'll be glad to wait on you."

"No, no. That won't be necessary." Her glance swept across

both of them, her lips pursed, her lashless eyes blinking fast and furious as they always did, as if sand had blown in them and she was trying to blink it away.

"They're serving lemonade," he said, holding out his cup. "Like they served at the social after Thanksgiving. Someone said Mrs. Hayes made a large batch of the delicious drink. Be sure and get some before it runs out, Mrs. Boutwell."

She didn't respond but instead turned to Sebbie. "It looks like you've been doing a lot of drinking this afternoon."

"Oh, no, Mrs. Boutwell," Sebbie remarked. "This is my first cup."

"I wasn't meaning that kind of drinking." Mrs. Boutwell peered intently into Sebbie's eyes and began to sing— loudly. " 'Drink to me only with thine eyes, and I will drink with mine.' "

Sebbie blushed scarlet as she fidgeted with her cup and nearly dropped it. The nerve of the woman! She was singing—loudly—the love ballad that described what Sebbie had been sitting there doing. Was it that visible to those around her? Her feelings of love for Griffin? Apparently so. But it was rude of Mrs. Boutwell to embarrass her in this manner. She righted her cup and sat as still as a sentinel, not knowing what to do, what to say, how to respond.

Griffin shot up. "Looks like Miss Hanford's cup is nearly empty." He took Sebbie's cup from her viselike grip. "If you'll excuse me, Mrs. Boutwell, I'll go refill it now."

Thank you, Griffin, Sebbie said with her eyes as she gazed up at him. *You rescued me.*

Mrs. Boutwell tsk-huffed. "Very well, Mr. Parks. I'd like a private word with Sebbie anyway. This is the perfect opportunity."

Sebbie grew hot all over. What could she do to ward off the cantankerous lady? She was as much a toad as her pitiful son, the young Mr. Boutwell. There. She'd said it, and she wasn't sorry for it. It was the truth. But what could she do to get away from the lady's unwanted company? Nothing, she knew. Proper decorum dictated she hear her out.

"Sebbie?" A look of concern was etched in Griffin's features as he leaned near her.

"I'll be happy to talk with you, Mrs. Boutwell," Sebbie said woodenly. "Give us a few moments, Griff—Mr. Parks?"

"Certainly." He turned on his heel and walked away.

Mrs. Boutwell plopped her plumpness into Griffin's chair, situated her skirts, and faced Sebbie. "I've something to tell you, Sebbie. Something very important."

Sebbie looked past Mrs. Boutwell, all the way across the room. Her gaze caught and held two little girls holding hands with Ophelia and Cecilia, the four of them playing ring-around-the-rosy, skipping and singing and shrieking with joy.

"I'm sure you'll be interested in hearing what I have to say."

Nothing could be further from the truth, Mrs. Boutwell. I don't think I'm interested in anything you have to say. Thrusting away her impatient thoughts, Sebbie looked patiently at the older woman.

Mrs. Boutwell ran her portly hands down her midsection and leaned close to Sebbie. "I hear you. . .uh. . .how shall I say this? I hear you dislike well-to-doers. That you have a disdain for them, in fact."

Sebbie was aghast. What was the woman's reason for saying something like this? What concern was it of hers? And how could she know this?

"And?" Sebbie tugged on her collar. One of her camellias fell down her bodice, and the stem stuck in her chest, but she said not a word, only thought long and hard.

"You don't care at all for rich people, right? You think they are pompous boors, correct?"

Sebbie felt as if she were being grilled during the Spanish Inquisition. What right did Mrs. Boutwell have to be doing this to her, asking her questions that made her feel uncomfortable?

Mrs. Boutwell gave out a throaty little laugh. "In a place this small, secrets are hard to keep."

Still, Sebbie said nothing. She simply didn't know how to respond.

"Cat got your tongue? My, my. I heard that little piece of information from a direct source, your feelings about well-to-doers—"

"Oh dear." Sebbie's thoughts ran amok. She and Griffin had had a discussion about well-heeled people, why they acted the way they did. They had been standing outside this very building one Sunday after service. She thought the area had been secluded where they stood near Marco Polo.

Apparently, she had thought wrong. A certain man flashed before her eyes. He had walked by and tipped his bowler hat at them as she and Griffin were conversing that day. The young Mr. Artemis Boutwell. Suddenly, Sebbie felt sick to her stomach. Had he eavesdropped? Most assuredly so.

"I'm not at liberty to say who told me this information." Mrs. Boutwell paused, as if she were waiting for Sebbie to make an admission.

"Mrs. Boutwell, I said—"

"No need to explain, Missy. I know exactly what you said." Mrs. Boutwell waved her lacy fan in front of her, the veins on her nostrils bright red and spiderlike. "Nonetheless, what's important is what I have to say next." She leaned so close, Sebbie could smell the dusting powder on her portly neck. She whispered into Sebbie's ear; and when she was through whispering, she stood up, a smug look on her face and her haughty nose high in the air as she made her way toward the refreshment table.

Sebbie sat there in a daze. Griffin? Well-heeled? Well-to-do? Wealthy? She recounted all the things Mrs. Boutwell had said, her thoughts running in a frenzy. Rich people, at least the ones she had met, were pompous, unfeeling boors. People like the young Mr. Artemis Boutwell. He certainly fit that description.

But her thoughts raced on. No, Griffin wasn't a pompous, unfeeling boor. Of course not. She had come to know him. She had come to love him. He was. . .he was wonderful.

Oh, Griffin, why didn't you tell me this?

She took a deep breath, willing herself to be calm. Mrs. Boutwell was trying to stir up trouble. She must be fibbing. That was it. She took pleasure in sowing unkind seeds.

But Mrs. Boutwell was the banker's wife. She would know these things. Hadn't Griffin said he did business at Mr. Boutwell's bank?

Sebbie rubbed her temples, her head suddenly throbbing with intensity, her thoughts aswirl.

"Here you are," Griffin said, holding out her cup. "Your lemonade. I managed to get the last ladleful. For you." His eyes were pools of affection.

"Thank you, Griffin. I'm sure it'll be. . .as delightful as my first cup."

She tried to hide the despondency in her voice.

She tried to hide the pain in her head.

She tried to hide the shaking in her hands.

But she didn't succeed.

"Aren't you feeling well, Sebbie?" Griffin looked at her with concern. He didn't wait for an answer. "Mrs. Boutwell." A look of disapproval crossed his face. "Her meddlesome ways are enough to turn an Aphrodite into a Medusa." He frowned. "She spreads discord and contentiousness everywhere she goes."

Sebbie felt the camellia stem in her bodice rake her skin. She had to get it out. She had to get herself out. Perhaps a breath of fresh air would help her. She stood up, sloshing her lemonade but not caring, a few drops hitting her skirts and leaving a trail. She would have to scrub the stain tonight before it set. She placed the cup on her chair with a clank. "I–I'll see you momentarily." She started walking across the hard wooden floor.

"Do you want me to find Kit?" he called after her. "Bertie? To assist you?"

"No." She stopped in her tracks. She owed him kindness. She turned, retraced her steps. She forced a smile. "It's nearly time to go. I probably need to help Mama corral the girlies."

He nodded. "People are gathering up their things and leaving."

"The party's almost over. . . ." Her voice trailed off, and she went in search of her mother.

&

"Mama, may I have a talk with you?" Sebbie asked at bed-time. She had just finished scrubbing out the lemonade in her blue silk dress, which she put over a line she had strung in the kitchen. "Are you too tired?"

"Of course not," her mother responded. "Come into my room when you're ready for bed."

A quarter hour later, Sebbie tiptoed into her mother's bedroom, being careful not to wake the twins in the trundle bed. She let out a soft *b-r-r-r-r* as she crossed the room in her bare feet.

"Come, Dear." Her mother patted the spot beside her in the wide bed, then threw back the blanket and sheets.

The lamp on the table flickered as Sebbie passed it.

"Go ahead and turn off the lamp. Might as well save the oil. And you might as well sleep in here too. No need to go traipsing back to your room through the cold."

Sebbie turned off the lamp, then dashed for the bed, threw off her wrapper, and climbed in.

Her mother let out a little gasp as Sebbie's feet touched

her legs. "Your feet are as cold as the pond we used to skate on up north."

Sebbie laughed.

"You just reminded me of something I miss about your papa."

Sebbie burrowed into the covers, situating her head against the feather pillow and pulling the blanket up to her chin. "What's that, Mama?" In the bedding, she smelled not the scent of lavender water many women wore. That was no longer a part of her mother's toilette. No, she smelled a whiff of good clean lye soap, and she breathed in deeply of the pleasantness. "What is it you miss about Papa?"

"My feet were always cold—like yours are tonight. He used to let me tuck them in the crook of his knees, and soon they were toasty warm."

Sebbie tucked hers in the crook of her mother's knees.

"Course he used to yelp and go on and on about it, saying I was freezing the daylights out of him. But I think he enjoyed it. It was our private little game."

Directly, Sebbie felt movement in the bed and knew her mother's shoulders were shaking. "Mama? You're not crying, are you?"

More movement. Her mother reaching for a handkerchief on the bedside table?

"Not now, I'm not."

"Oh, Mama. Don't cry."

"Soon, you'll understand. When you've experienced the love between a husband and wife."

Sebbie nodded. "I–I feel so sad when you cry."

"It's been a long time since I did that."

"I'm glad. You're our rock, Mama, and we need you to be strong for us."

"Yes. . ."

"I love you, Mama."

"I love you, Dear." Her mother drew a deep breath and

slowly released it. "Now." She paused. "I promise I can talk about your papa without crying." She let out a little laugh. "Jed could brighten any corner. I loved him so dearly. We had such happy times together. We used to lie in bed like this at night, talking about the day's events, talking about the ranch, talking about the children, talking about anything that came to our minds, even joshing a trifle. Now God has given you a good man. Soon, you'll be married to Griffin, and you'll be lying in bed with him like Jed and I used to do."

Sebbie was glad it was dark. Her face would be scarlet red. She lay there as quiet as a mouse, Mama chattering on, not hearing a word her mother said, thoughts of Griffin filling her mind. . . .

"Marriage is a wonderful partnership," her mother was saying. "But here I am, going on and on, and you asked to talk with me. What is it you want to say, Sebbie? Your feet are warm now. Don't you want to put your knees down?"

Sebbie stretched her legs out straight, then turned over and faced Mama. She raised up on her elbow. A shaft of moonlight shone across the covers, the windowpanes making a cross pattern atop it, and she traced it with her finger.

"What is it you want to talk about, Dear? You seemed a little troubled at the end of the party today. Is everything all right between you and Griffin?"

"Oh, Mama, Mrs. Boutwell said he's. . .well-to-do. He's not just a cowhand."

At first, her mother didn't respond, so unlike her talkative self.

Long moments of silence passed, and Sebbie wondered if her mother had dozed off. After all, she'd had a day filled with excitement. They all had. She decided to venture and see if her mother was asleep. "Mama? What do you think I should do? About Griffin? When I found out, I was hurt that he didn't tell me this about himself. Mama? Did you hear me?"

"I'm sorry. I was thinking instead of talking. That's a good thing to do sometimes, don't you think?" She let out her happy little laugh. "Do you know what I was thinking, Dear?"

"No. What?"

"I was thinking that he must've had a good reason."

Sebbie traced the cross pattern again. "I'm thinking you're right, Mama."

"Do you know what else I was thinking?"

"No, Mama."

"I was thinking about a Scripture passage: 'Ask, and it shall be given you. . . .what man is there of you, whom if his son ask bread, will he give him a stone? Or if he ask a fish, will he give him a serpent? If ye then, being evil, know how to give good gifts unto your children, how much more shall your Father which is in heaven give good things to them that ask him?' Sebbie, do you remember what I asked God for a few months ago?"

"That He would provide a husband of means for me? To help our family?"

"Yes. It appears God has answered my prayer."

The familiar tingles crawled up Sebbie's spine, her thoughts on Griffin again. She turned over on her back and pulled the covers up to her chin. A scent of good clean soap wafted through the air, and she sighed contentedly.

Mama quoted more Scripture verses about God answering prayer. " 'Let us therefore come boldly unto the throne of grace, that we may obtain mercy, and find grace to help in time of need.' 'The eyes of the LORD are upon the righteous, and his ears are open unto their cry.' "

Sebbie let out another sigh of contentment. "Hallelujah!"

twenty-one

On Christmas day, Sebbie helped her mother prepare for their late afternoon Christmas dinner. They all worked with a vengeance. Even Kit and Bertie helped in the hustle and bustle.

Griffin is coming, Griffin is coming, Griffin is coming, Sebbie's heart sang.

There was the dressing to make and the turkey to roast. Kit had happened upon a wild gobbler the day before, and they had all been as pleased as could be. Otherwise, it would be baked chicken, which was good, but not quite the same as a turkey. Then there were potatoes to be peeled and boiled, and gravy to make, and a cake to bake, and a custard to be whipped up. Jars of green beans and corn needed to be opened and heated up. Light-as-a-cloud biscuits with butter and jelly would round out the meal.

Oh, we're having a grand supper, Sebbie thought with glee as she stirred together corn bread makings to be used for the dressing.

They had to make the house ready too. Though it was always clean and stood at the ready for anyone who happened by, it still needed to have its daily sweeping and dusting. The yard should be raked, and then of course there were the daily chores that no one gave a thought to, like the milking and the water drawing.

The girlies were underfoot and dissatisfied all morning until Sebbie set them to making cut-out stars for the Christmas tree. All afternoon as everyone worked, the girlies worked too. Soon, there were enough stars to decorate two trees.

Then it was time to wash and dress with haste and wash

and dress the girlies and get back to dinner fixings.

Sebbie's heart gave a joyful little start when she heard a knock at the front door. *Griffin!*

The first one to it, she swung the door wide open, and he stood facing her, laden with presents and packages. His eyes said, *I love you,* and hers said the wonderful phrase back.

Later, they all sat down and ate. Griffin proclaimed it the best Christmas dinner he'd ever eaten. Mama offered a polite thank-you, Kit and Bertie beamed, the girlies grinned, and Sebbie smiled quietly.

After dessert, they gathered in the parlor, and as on the night he first came to Happy Acres, they sang to the accompaniment of Sebbie's piano playing, only this time they chose favorite Christmas carols.

Mama designated the task of lighting the Christmas tree to Kit and Bertie. With the care and precision their mother had taught them through the years, they lit each candle as all looked on, until the room gave off a happy glow in the pine-scented air.

Then Mama picked up the Bible and asked Griffin to read the Christmas story from Luke, and she followed up with prayer.

Griffin asked if he could pass out the presents he had brought; and Mama acquiesced, although first she protested demurely that it wasn't necessary for him to give them gifts. But he simply replied that it gave him pleasure and to please accept the gifts graciously.

When he gave out the presents to the girls and girlies, they exclaimed over their gifts, each well suited to their tastes. The twins were enthralled with the two identical dolls from Hayes's General Store.

Mama let out a peal of glee when she opened her present— threads of multitudinous colors, a large packet of needles, and a brand-new pair of scissors, all nestled in a deluxe sewing box.

When Sebbie folded back the wrapper of her gift, she

thought she surely would faint. Her treasured lengths of wedding silk! Shimmering in the candle glow, their satiny sentiments seemed to call out to her, and she thought her heart would burst from happiness.

"Oh, Griffin," she whispered. But she could say no more. She just stared down at the silk, not touching it lest it get mussed. When she started crying, she pulled the paper over the material so her tears wouldn't stain it. Griffin touched her forearm, and their gazes locked, and it seemed as if they were the only ones in the room, so sweet was the love that flowed between them.

"May I share something with you?" Griffin asked, looking first at Mama and then at each person seated around the room. In the sudden quietness, everyone seemed keenly attuned to him, even the girlies.

"Certainly, Griffin," Mama said.

"A year ago, I prayed that God would give me a wife, a woman who would love me for who I am and not for what I can give her." He picked up the Bible that he had laid aside, opened it to Genesis, and read the love story of Isaac and Rebekah.

"When I first met Sebbie," he said when he was done reading, "she was standing beside the well—right out there." He pointed in the direction of the well in the yard. "From that very moment, I sensed she was everything I desired— sweet, talented, gracious, and beautiful besides. When she gave me some water, I wondered if she was the girl I was looking for. And then when she offered to water my horse, well, I guess the best way to put it is, I lost my heart to her."

Kit sighed.

Bertie fluttered her eyelashes.

The twins giggled.

Mama smiled, her hand over her heart.

"I was deeply touched that Sebbie agreed to board Marco

Polo for me. And when she sacrificed her wedding silk. . ."
He gestured to the package on the low table in front of him
and slowly shook his head.

In a flash, he was on his knees in front of Sebbie.

Kit sighed again.

Bertie couldn't stop fluttering her eyelashes.

The twins giggled uproariously.

Mama smiled all the more.

And Sebbie thought surely she had died and gone to glory.

Griffin took Sebbie's hand in his. He leaned forward and
kissed the back of it; and as his lips brushed her skin, she
thought she was going to swoon.

"Sebbie, may I have your hand in marriage?" he asked, his
eyes never leaving hers.

Her heart didn't just sing as she sat there gazing at him. It
shouted, *Hallelujah!* "Like Rebekah of old, I am willing,
Griffin. More than willing."

" 'And Isaac brought her into his mother Sarah's tent,' " he
quoted from the Bible, his deep bass voice a mere whisper.
" 'And took Rebekah, and she became his wife; and he loved
her.' " He rose from the divan, pulled Sebbie to her feet, and
wrapped his arms around her.

As she lost herself in the kiss that followed, the only way
Sebbie could think of to describe it was "almost heaven."

A Letter To Our Readers

Dear Reader:

In order that we might better contribute to your reading enjoyment, we would appreciate your taking a few minutes to respond to the following questions. We welcome your comments and read each form and letter we receive. When completed, please return to the following:

Fiction Editor
Heartsong Presents
PO Box 719
Uhrichsville, Ohio 44683

1. Did you enjoy reading *The Tender Heart* by Kristy Dykes?
   ❏ Very much! I would like to see more books by this author!
   ❏ Moderately. I would have enjoyed it more if

   _____

   _____

   _____

2. Are you a member of **Heartsong Presents**? ❏ Yes ❏ No
   If no, where did you purchase this book? _____

   _____

3. How would you rate, on a scale from 1 (poor) to 5 (superior), the cover design? _____

4. On a scale from 1 (poor) to 10 (superior), please rate the following elements.

   ____ Heroine   ____ Plot
   ____ Hero   ____ Inspirational theme
   ____ Setting   ____ Secondary characters

5. These characters were special because?_____

_____

_____

6. How has this book inspired your life?_____

_____

_____

7. What settings would you like to see covered in future
   Heartsong Presents books? _____

_____

_____

8. What are some inspirational themes you would like to see
   treated in future books? _____

_____

_____

9. Would you be interested in reading other **Heartsong
   Presents** titles? ❑ Yes ❑ No

10. Please check your age range:
    ❑ Under 18   ❑ 18-24
    ❑ 25-34   ❑ 35-45
    ❑ 46-55   ❑ Over 55

Name _____

Occupation _____

Address _____

City_____ State_____ Zip_____

CHURCH IN THE WILDWOOD

4 stories in 1

*F*or four generations, the citizens of Hickory Hollow, Missouri, have gathered for worship in the valley's little brown church. Many a soul has found salvation amid this blissful country scene. . .and more than a few lonely hearts have met their true love while seated on the chapel's pew.

Authors: Paige Winship Dooly, Kristy Dykes, Pamela Griffin, and Debby Mayne.

Historical, paperback, 352 pages, 5 ³/₁₆"x 8"

❤ ❤ ❤ ❤ ❤ ❤ ❤ ❤ ❤ ❤ ❤ ❤ ❤ ❤ ❤

Please send me _____ copies of *Church in the Wildwood* I am enclosing $6.97 for each. (Please add $2.00 to cover postage and handling per order. OH add 7% tax.)

Send check or money order, no cash or C.O.D.s please.

Name _____

Address _____

City, State, Zip _____

To place a credit card order, call 1-800-847-8270.

Send to: Heartsong Presents Reader Service, PO Box 721, Uhrichsville, OH 44683

❤ ❤ ❤ ❤ ❤ ❤ ❤ ❤ ❤ ❤ ❤ ❤ ❤ ❤ ❤

Heartsong

Presents

Great Inspirational Romance at a Great Price!

Heartsong Presents books are inspirational romances in contemporary and historical settings, designed to give you an enjoyable, spirit-lifting reading experience. You can choose wonderfully written titles from some of today's best authors like Peggy Darty, Sally Laity, Tracie Peterson, Colleen L. Reece, Debra White Smith, and many others.

When ordering quantities less than twelve, above titles are $3.25 each.
Not all titles may be available at time of order.